T0383287

TWELVE
POST-WAR
TALES

TWELVE
POST-WAR
TALES

Graham Swift

SCRIBNER

London · New York · Amsterdam/Antwerp · Sydney/Melbourne · Toronto · New Delhi

This edition published in Great Britain by Scribner,
an imprint of Simon & Schuster UK Ltd, 2025

1 3 5 7 9 10 8 6 4 2

Simon & Schuster UK Ltd, 1st Floor
222 Gray's Inn Road, London WC1X 8HB

Simon & Schuster Australia, Sydney
Simon & Schuster India, New Delhi

www.simonandschuster.co.uk
www.simonandschuster.com.au
www.simonandschuster.co.in

The authorised representative in the EEA is Simon & Schuster Netherlands BV,
Herculesplein 96, 3584 AA Utrecht, Netherlands. info@simonandschuster.nl

Simon & Schuster strongly believes in freedom of expression and stands against
censorship in all its forms. For more information, visit BooksBelong.com.

A CIP catalogue record for this book is available from the British Library

Hardback ISBN: 978-1-3985-3548-0
eBook ISBN: 978-1-3985-3549-7
eAudio ISBN: 978-1-3985-3550-3

Typeset in Garamond by M Rules
Printed and Bound in the UK using 100% Renewable
Electricity at CPI Group (UK) Ltd

CONTENTS

For Candice

The fundamental things apply
As time goes by

Herman Hupfeld: *As Time Goes By*, song, 1931

I

THE NEXT BEST THING

THE NEXT BEST THING

It hardly warranted his personal attention, but since his English was considered fluent—even sometimes 'perfect'—and since it might involve an appointment with a British serviceman, Herr Büchner had decided he should handle the matter directly. It had anyway landed on his desk, as many things did that were not addressed to any specific person, in the form of a letter from the man's commanding officer, a Major Wilkes, written, as it happened, in rather poor German.

How fitting that it should have fallen under the eye of a man with (almost) perfect English.

Certain useful English expressions had come quickly and

freshly to Herr Büchner's mind, such as 'wrong channels' or 'knocking on the wrong door'. But since the circumstances were peculiar—this wasn't a German citizen, it was one of the Allieds—and since the thing had the backing, as it were, of the British Army . . .

After reading the letter and looking through the enclosures, including the sobering list of names, he had sighed and pondered. He could recognise self-righteous pomposity when he saw it. He didn't like being ordered about, even indirectly, by this Major Wilkes, as if he were under the man's command himself. This was Germany in 1959, not 1949. And his was only a department at the *Rathaus*.

'To whom it may concern.' Well.

True, it was the constant business of his department, almost, he sometimes felt, its principal task, to receive enquiries and applications that were none of its business and to—politely, patiently and efficiently—redirect them. He might have written a reply to Major Wilkes, in excellent English of course, in the sort of chilly English the English were so good at, informing him, if not in such blunt language, that he was indeed knocking on the wrong door and that the *Rathaus*, as Major Wilkes should know, didn't handle such stuff. And generally reminding him, if not in so many words, that Germany was not an occupied country any more.

4

Herr Büchner could see that this might have been a justifiable response. But he could also see—he sighed again—that the correct response was to put on a show of exemplary co-operation, and that this should perhaps include his receiving in his office, even with something like servility, the subject of the letter, the man himself.

And now the man himself, a Private Joseph Caan, from London N8, currently residing with the British Army of the Rhine, was before him, plainly unnerved to be greeted by an *Amtsleiter* who yet spoke alarmingly crisp English, and plainly trying but failing to equate this interview with the one—demanding enough—he must previously have had with his 'CO', Major Wilkes.

Plainly out of his depth, yet out of his depth—this aroused Herr Büchner's interest—of his own choosing.

'Won't you sit down, Mr Caan?'

He shook the man's hand in a routine way, but eyed him with a friendly smile. He had chosen the 'Mr', which might of course only have confused, but this was a civil institution and he was eager to put the man at ease, if not actually to say, 'At ease.' Wasn't that the British Army rigmarole? 'At ease.' Then 'Stand easy.'

'I'm not your commanding officer.' He smiled again.

'You don't have to stand to attention.' He had tried to control his tone. He had stood, himself, to greet the man, then gestured to the chair in front of his desk before resuming his own seat.

'Won't you take off your beret?'

Herr Büchner was more than twice the man's age, and had been a soldier himself. It was long ago, but he retained from his military days the view that some men, perhaps most men, could both be and look like soldiers, even look as if soldiers were what they were meant to be; but some men could never look like, let alone *be* soldiers, even if, unfortunately, soldiers were what they were. He very quickly put Private Caan—Mr Caan—in the latter category. He once would have put himself in it, though this man before him might not have thought so. If, indeed, such thoughts ever occurred to him.

But perhaps they were occurring to him right now. Wasn't it still the standard repeated thought of any British conscript doing his time in Germany: What had this smarmy bastard done in the war?

The man took off his beret, revealing short, curled, springing dark hair, which caused Herr Büchner to recall the English expression 'short and curlies', almost exclusively used, he remembered, with the phrase 'got you by'.

6

Herr Büchner—Hans Büchner—retained, too, from his military days the view that a great many things happened in life that were beyond your control and might even be aimed at taking control from you—for example, if you were on the wrong side of a desk—but even when they happened in circumstances within your control, they really only happened, and whole futures might depend on it, because either you liked the look of the man's face in front of you or you didn't.

Private Caan's face was likeable because he didn't look like a soldier. Nor did he look, really, like a 'Mr'. Would he normally be known as 'Joe'? He looked like a boy. He was only nineteen. Along with the curly dark hair, he had small dark eyes that peered effortfully in a way that suggested a need for spectacles or just for general clarity, but, plainly, hadn't earned him an exemption on the grounds of a failed eye test.

The scant details in the file opened on Herr Büchner's desk gave the man's civilian occupation as 'tailor's apprentice'. Close work—from the age of fifteen or so—with a needle? But the eyes when they finally met his own were not feeble. They were even a little 'needling'.

The expressions all came back.

Joseph Benjamin Caan. Mother's name, Eva Adele—maiden name, Rosenbaum. Father, Benjamin Franz—deceased.

Major Wilkes had seen fit to point out: 'killed in action in North Africa'.

Joe Caan, son of Ben Caan, from London N8.

The list that was the real matter in hand was mainly Caans and Rosenbaums. There was a Jakob, a Leopold, a Hanna, a Leah, a Bruno, an Elsa, a Ruben ... There was even a Hans. They had mostly been, it seemed, residents of Hanover.

Major Wilkes had also seen fit to point out that Private Caan's 'intentions' were in accordance with his mother's wishes, the implication being, Herr Büchner supposed, that the man was carrying out a task conferred on him by at least one elder and better.

But that suddenly sharp, not-to-be-fooled gaze told him otherwise. Private Caan might have said this was the case, so as to give his intentions already solid backing; or Major Wilkes might have asked him, pushily, if it were the case, because he couldn't just let any soldier go skiving off after some trumped-up personal matter. And Private Caan had wisely said that yes, of course, it was because his mother wished it.

But—bollocks. Herr Büchner used, to himself, another well-remembered and suddenly very serviceable English expression. Herr Büchner was a fairly shrewd judge of faces. The mother, Eva Adele, hadn't put her son up to it, he felt sure. The mother, who would perhaps, like himself, be in her early forties, would rather forget the whole thing, push it out of her mind—the easiest and sometimes the best option. It was just unlucky for her that her son had first of all been called up, then been sent to Germany. Of all places. This was the nub of the matter before him, and hadn't this Major Wilkes also seen it in this man's face?

It was rather unlucky for the son, too, but the son couldn't get out of it. It was where most of them got sent. Hadn't both mother and son even reckoned on it? And of course there would have been the other, perhaps equally troubling factor: the son was now a soldier, just like his father, Benjamin Franz—born in Germany but apparently killed in the British Army.

It was all interesting. He would have liked to have a conversation with this Private Caan, just a free and leisurely conversation, and here in his undisturbed office was the ideal opportunity; but it was not the matter at hand. Nor was it possible anyway, since the man before him clearly had very limited powers of conversation. If not of initiative.

He would have liked to say, with the right kind of smile, 'Your commanding officer has quite a command of German . . .'

Private Caan wasn't acting under his mother's orders, he'd give him that. It was all in those eyes. He wasn't a 'mother's boy', as the English say. He was probably about as far from his mother right now as he'd ever been. True, he might not have been sent to Germany at all, and then the matter would not have come up. He might have been sent to Hong Kong. But here he was, and here he'd be for several months, and Joseph Caan had decided he had to face the consequences—the 'music', as the English also say.

The man had taken off his beret promptly, as if ordered, but seemed not to know what to do with it. He clutched it in both hands, squeezing it like some comforting toy. Something had come into his life, something big and pressing, unlike perhaps anything that had come into his life before, and Joseph Caan had decided, all by himself, that he wasn't going to duck out of it. He wasn't going to allow his future self to say, when it would be for ever too late: You went to Germany, didn't you, you were in Germany, weren't you, and you never did anything. You prick.

The words came back—the words of English soldiers. And didn't this young man have a perfect right and reason to wonder what this smarmy bastard—or 'prick' too—had done in the war? Though how tripped-up he now seemed, to be addressed by a German in English better than his own.

Private Caan, though he was a soldier constantly required to obey orders, was acting, if very awkwardly, by himself, for himself. Herr Büchner could see that. He liked not only his face, he liked *him*.

But it was all very depressing. What could he, head of his department as he was, actually do for him? Might they not simply have a conversation? If Herr Büchner had smoked, he might have offered this man a cigarette. But he'd given up smoking when he'd returned to Germany, years ago. Smoking—if you could get cigarettes—had been all about killing time. He might invite the man to smoke anyway. Was that a pack of ten nestling in his breast pocket? 'Player's Please.'

Herr Büchner remembered when, long ago in another age, he'd just become an officer. A real officer, not a cadet, an officer of the most junior sort, but an officer. He hadn't anticipated the invisible threshold he'd still have to cross, the test he'd still have to undergo. If he was an officer, then he must act like one.

A man was standing before him. It was a moment just like this one, though it wasn't in an office in a town hall and the man really was standing rigidly to attention with no option to sit. And though the man was many years Hans Büchner's senior, he'd been obliged to salute and stamp his feet because he was before an officer, who was sitting at the time at a little desk, a good deal smaller and plainer than this present one, and might have looked like a boy in detention.

He hadn't anticipated being in a position of judgement, with the power to exercise either pitilessness or mercy, of being like God Almighty.

It was a trivial matter. The man would have liked, for convincingly pressing personal reasons, an extra day's leave. It was not an unreasonable request, and leniency would have been simple. Yet because Hans Büchner was an officer and had only just become one, he was not to be seen as a push-over. So he'd curtly dismissed the man's request, then told him he was dismissed himself.

Why? The man—he even remembered his name was Krüger—would hate him now. And he would hate himself, he would continue to hate himself. He wouldn't forget the moment—he couldn't forget it now—even when immeasurably worse things had come his way. His priggish little flaunting of power.

That was over twenty years ago. In Koblenz. And, years before then, he'd said to himself: Enlist, sign up, even while you're still at school. Choose before you're chosen. That way, you might be selected as an officer. That had been his covertly defensive line of thinking. See everything as an opportunity—that is, as a path always turning towards the minimum ultimate danger. 'Play your cards right', as the English put it.

And how cards had got played, again and again, to kill time, in sodden, rain-swept Lincolnshire. He might never have known there was such a place. Till the cards themselves became damp and tattered, each in their own forlorn way, till you could recognise every single one of them—if you were clever, if you played your cards right—without having to turn them over.

The man still clutched his beret. He seemed unable to transfer it, rolled up in the regular fashion, to his shoulder strap. Nor, it seemed, could he relax, sit back and cross his legs. Though how did you do that, with any sort of naturalness, in those thunderous boots and those ridiculous things—what were they called? 'Gaiters'? Yes, 'gaiters'.

How demeaning it must be, even for an *apprentice* tailor, to be shoved into the calamity of an outfit that was the standard British soldier's uniform. That absurdity called a 'battledress'.

'Please smoke if you wish, Mr Caan.' And he pushed an ashtray to within his reach.

But the man said, 'That's all right.' Which Herr Büchner knew was, in this case, English for, 'No, I won't, thanks.' Not, 'Yes, thanks, I will.'

Overawed as he was to find himself in such municipal (and German) surroundings, Private Caan was clearly expecting that after some 'buttering up'—already happening—he was about to be 'fobbed off'. A standard procedure in life.

And how right he might have been. And how little, perhaps, Private Caan would ever know how matters had tilted in his favour.

'You must understand, Mr Caan—pardon me for putting this so directly—but you have come, you have been sent by your superiors, to the wrong place. Matters of this kind are not dealt with locally, on a basis of proximity. This is just an ordinary *Rathaus*—town hall. This is just its regular Records Department. Downstairs, you will have passed what you would call a Registry Office. "Births, deaths and marriages." Your country always puts it in that strange order, I think.'

So there we are! The man's eyes had suddenly flared. He might have known it—Joseph Caan might have known it! He'd turned up on the dot of eleven, as if to be on parade. He'd had to seek permission, and no doubt make special arrangements to get here from his base outside town. Now, even in fancy English (Herr Büchner remembered the word 'poncy'), he was indeed being fobbed off. 'Given the brush off', the 'run around'.

It all came rushing back.

'Matters of this kind are not even dealt with by the German central government, by the *Bundesarchiv*, they are dealt with—as your commanding officer should know—by the Tracing Service, the *Suchdienst*. In Arolsen, near Kassel. The Tracing Service is not even a German institution, it is run by the International Red Cross.' (He might have added, 'As your mother, if she really wished to do something, might have found out long ago.') 'You should apply to the Tracing Service, that is the proper channel for enquiries like yours.'

But he had made the man suffer enough. Now it was the moment for leniency.

'Nonetheless ... nonetheless ...'

How he had always liked those lumbering English conjunctions, 'nonetheless', 'nevertheless' ...

'Nonetheless, since you are here, or rather since you are with the local garrison, since your freedom is restricted and since your request comes with the full support of your CO, I will do—I will be happy to do, Mr Caan—what I can for you on your behalf.' He re-engaged his welcoming smile. 'That is, I will contact the Tracing Service for you. I have some connections. And I will do what I can for you to find out the—fate—of your relatives.'

He hoped his smile was now fully benign, even a little melting. 'Fate' was an awkward word to fling into any conversation. Yet it was a highly adaptable and wide-ranging word. Fate, as in the turning over of a card, or the signing of a document, or a curt dismissal, or the pointing of a gun. Or—how many had once been doomed or saved?—the mere flicking of a finger.

The man now visibly altered. He betrayed the fact that until this point he had been in a state of considerable tension and apprehension. He said, 'Thank you, sir,' almost like some excused wrongdoer.

It was a good word, 'thank you', a better word than 'fate'.

'Please—I don't need the "sir". I am a public servant, I should be the one to call you "sir". I will do what I can, I assure you. And whatever I can ascertain I will pass on to you, by writing to your commanding officer. I think that is the proper channel, don't you? But I must warn you that what I can find out, as I'm sure you will understand, may be very little. It may be little more than what—if I can put it this way—you may imagine already. Remarkably detailed records do exist. It is both shocking and useful that they exist. On the other hand, a great deal was destroyed, you will understand, towards the end of the war.'

The man was now looking at him still gratefully, but with those sharpening eyes again.

'One thing I will say to you, Mr Caan, if I may ... Whatever I may discover, whatever I may be able to pass on to you, I recommend that you follow through the matter yourself, while you are here in Germany, if you can. I recommend that you go to the Tracing Service yourself and see what there is, and talk to the people there. It is some distance from here of course. There is the issue of getting the appropriate permission and assistance—but you have already got this far. I leave that with you and your superiors. But you have my own assistance for now. In some matters, Mr Caan, I think it is important, while you have the opportunity, not to hold back, but to meet the thing—I think you would say "head on". I'm sure you understand. You have already begun to meet it. Quite commendably, if I may say so.'

There. And spoken to a soldier. Now the man would even feel virtuous and justified. On a Thursday morning, in an ordinary German *Rathaus*, he might even feel rather heroic. Even if nothing more of substance transpired, he might always tell himself: I was in Germany and I didn't simply sit on my arse.

He might even tell his mother one day.

And he might meanwhile tell his commanding officer (but this was Herr Büchner's unspoken fantasy) that it was not for any British officer to snap his fingers at the local authorities any more and 'keep them on their toes' and 'make them jump to it'. Or imply such things in inept German.

Good God, Germany was actually starting to pick itself up, hadn't this Major Wilkes noticed? And it was these poor creatures—his men—in their battledresses, once the swaggering conquerors, who were starting to resemble so many refugees, stuck out there in their wretched camp. What must their famous Great Britain look like these days?

Herr Büchner wished this man was a conversationalist, so he could ask him that question directly and frankly. But it was plain that, for whatever reason—perhaps no more than having had to obey for several months the soldierly rule of only speaking when spoken to—Private Caan was not a talker. A thinker maybe, not a talker.

And he, Herr Büchner, or Herr Leutnant Büchner as he

was then, had once had plenty of time—and might not this man take a mental leap and guess?—to see what their Great Britain looked like. At least in those days. Plenty of time to get used to their 'Now look here, my man's and their 'Now listen here, my good chap's.

But it was his last chance, and he didn't want to just 'dismiss' this man.

'I would offer you a cup of coffee, Mr Caan, if it was in my power. But as you'll now be aware, the *Rathaus* isn't a place of great luxury.' He smiled and raised his hands in apology. 'But a little better, I hope, than a barracks.'

'That's all right.'

The man kneaded his beret. And of course: how frightening, soldier as he was, to have to take coffee with an *Amtsleiter*. Let alone have a conversation.

'Well then, I have your—list. But if there should be any other details you are able—might wish—to add . . . ?'

Herr Büchner eyed again the sheet of paper, the names before him. Jakob, Leopold, Hanna . . . This man would have known little enough about them, he could never have met any of them. Against some was a once-known (now doubtless defunct) address, a guessed-at occupation. 'Tailor?' 'Jeweller?' 'Leather goods dealer?' The scant particulars weren't so much thinner than those that came with

Joseph Caan. But the most important particular was of course self-evident.

What a terrible thing in itself could be just a list of names. Major Wilkes, when enclosing it, might have thought: So there!

'Your CO mentions that your father was killed in North Africa.'

He said it casually, as if he'd only just noticed it while rereading what was before him and not registered it, on first perusal, as provocative. It, too, was no doubt meant to deliver its 'So there!' Its 'So you'd better bloody jump to it!'

And no doubt this Major Wilkes had once done something praiseworthy in Normandy or, God knows, crossing the Rhine.

'Yes,' Private Caan simply said.

Herr Büchner had the impression that he'd tried to make this 'yes' sound as neutral as possible.

He smiled at him again, hoping that his smile—it was all so complicated—would not seem in any way patronising.

'Then I must tell you that I also served in North Africa. On the other side, of course.'

There. He tried to gauge the expression on the man's face. It looked no more than perplexed—and young. But at least he'd now given Joseph Caan part of the answer to that unspoken question: What had this prick done in the war?

And had he even graduated from being a prick? Herr Büchner hoped so.

'Is your father, is he—at rest, buried—in North Africa?'

What a challenging thing, indeed, was a conversation.

'In Tobruk.'

'Tobruk.'

How the word dropped suddenly into Herr Büchner's office. Then tumbled, heavily and abruptly, from his own mouth. He'd always thought that it sounded like some piece of broken masonry, like another word for 'rubble'. It even sounded rather German.

But he didn't say to the man before him—and he couldn't have said why he didn't say it—that he'd been at Tobruk himself, or very close to it. When, of course, it had been under German siege.

He didn't say it. Might he regret not saying it? Would it be like failing to do the very thing he'd recommended: meeting the thing 'head on'? He'd simply echoed the word clumsily, as if he might be learning it for the first time.

Fate: a very awkward thing altogether.

And this man's father had also been on the 'other side', if the expression now made any sense. That is—it was simple deduction—a German, turned British, fighting against Germans. As well as a Jew.

'Tobruk,' Herr Büchner said. 'I see.'

Why had he said no more? Could not this man help him—take up the loose end, the thrown rope even, of this stumbling exchange? But he was only nineteen and to be tongue-tied seemed his natural condition, even when another before him was uncharacteristically tongue-tied too.

The lump of a word had filled Herr Büchner's mouth. When had he last spoken it?

He got up, signalling that the appointment was over and held out his hand—less routinely, he hoped—once more.

'Well, you may leave it with me. And I'll be in touch. Through your commanding officer of course.'

Then the man left, recovering proper control at last of his beret and restoring it to his head. There was, fortunately, no automatic impulse to salute. When he emerged through the main entrance into the *Platz* outside he would no doubt take a good lungful of air and feel gratified and released. If nothing at all now happened, he might feel he had done his duty, to himself, had satisfied his conscience and had even honoured his missing, murdered kin.

And his mother may or may not be any the wiser.

Herr Büchner sat down again at his desk, his hands on the still open file. He had put up his hands once in North Africa and that was that. He had received his ticket, his acquittal, his alibi, call it what you like. His hands were clean—and Africa would even become known as 'the clean war'. In fact, his hands, his face, his eyes, his ears, his uniform to the point of obliteration, were covered in dust. His mouth, even, was full of dust. He'd never thought it was possible to be so caked with dust.

He had received his exit, his permission of leave, just as Herr and Frau Caan—Mr and Mrs Caan to-be—must have received their permission of leave some twenty years and more ago, taking the boat, from Bremerhaven or wherever, to London. Two of the lucky ones.

He, Hans Büchner, would eventually be put on a boat himself, one of the lucky ones too, and end up also in England, or Great Britain, whichever you preferred. In Lincolnshire, as it eventually turned out. And what was Lincolnshire like? It was not like Africa. It was green for a start and often very wet. And every night, though not when it was very wet, the bombers massed overhead, before crossing the sea, just to remind them, it sometimes seemed, down below in their huts, that their country was getting 'what-for'. That was the expression used: 'what-for'.

And one night one of those same bombers, possibly, had released its bombs on Mannheim, or rather somewhere near enough, and that's how—it would be a long time before he'd know it—his mother and father, Ernst and Clara Büchner, as fate would have it, had died, in 1943, in the village not far from Mannheim where Ernst Büchner had been the pastor.

But he, their son Hans, was out of it, none of it had anything to do with him. He had his POW certificate of exemption. He could still feel, even now, those initials like a brand upon him—Pee-Oh-Double-You—as he could still feel that choking dust in his mouth. As he could feel now the word Tobruk—it was not unlike the word *kaputt*—jarring against his tongue. The only cost, the only price of his certificate was six years of his life, his youth, the 'best years of your life' as they say.

But tell this to those who had suffered far worse.

If he'd been really shrewd—practised spotter of opportunity as he was—he might have formed some risky liaison with a farmer's daughter and gone into what? The pig trade? He might have turned totally native and become English, or British, himself.

But, as it was, at the end of one of the huts was a little section with shelves of books and even a workable stove. Good God, a library. Supplied by whom? What kind or stupid soul had thought that a shipment of German officers might want an offering of books, in English? A little propagandist taste of English literature. Dr Johnson. *Pride and Prejudice.*

So, while the rain poured down, he took the opportunity to improve, to master his English, supposing that one day, when the thing was over, this might be another kind of ticket. There must have been not a few like him.

All around him in the camp and when they were put to work in the fields—in Lincolnshire, even with 'a war on', you were never short of potatoes—was the common or filthy stuff and in the books was the cream. He acquired, in six years, almost immaculate (and when necessary, filthy) English, though what good had it, in fact, done him when he finally got home?

Until now perhaps, until this day, this ordinary overcast Thursday. His English had had the chance to blossom, to shine, to come into its own.

And had come up against an Englishman close to mute.

One day, in Lincolnshire, they had been briskly told that Adolf Hitler was dead, that Berlin was flattened, that something unspeakable had been discovered near the small town of Bergen. So there.

One day, or rather night, the bombers stopped flying.

But it would be another two years, and so much the better perhaps, before they were returned; and when they returned they were frightened, truly frightened—and rightly—at what they might find. Then several more years, like another imprisonment all over again, of being part of the national penance. Though their hands were clean. Look, perfectly clean.

But what had he discovered, even to his surprise? That he was a German, that's what, and this was where he belonged. This was his long-lost home. Even though his actual home, along with his parents, was long gone; this was the place where he was born.

He stood and went to the window, from where he knew he'd be able to see Private Caan crossing the square, pausing for the trams. And there he was. He wondered how much Joseph Caan would remember this day, if it would stay with him, if it would always matter. If he'd remember, when he'd been a soldier once, crossing a German square— Karlsplatz—and feeling briefly not like a soldier (if he'd ever felt that), but, just for a while, despite the uniform, like a free young man. All his life ahead of him.

The English had that odd little guessing rhyme: Tinker, tailor, soldier . . .

Yes, people kept coming still to the *Rathaus*, to his

department, wanting to find out, wanting to know, and having to be told that it was not the business of the *Rathaus*. They should apply to the *Suchdienst*, weren't they aware of that? Here—here is a leaflet with the details.

Still they came, though it was 1959, and this was only one town. The evidence even seemed to be that *more* of them were coming forward now. Perhaps it took some plucking up, some confronting. Or perhaps in recent years there'd been so much else to do, to be getting on with. Or perhaps the passage of time simply posed an ever more pressing question: If not now, when? Are you ever going to do it, are you going to let your life slip by—*your* life—and never—?

He watched Private Caan reach the other side of the square and disappear beyond the new row of lindens.

Of course you could simply do nothing, turn your back, forget, live. It was a choice.

No, it wasn't their job here at the *Rathaus*, he would say, but always politely and sympathetically, and always with his recommendation (though what should he, Hans Büchner, know about it?) that if they were going to take it further, then they should *really* take it further. Head on. Why did he say this?

It was not a matter of mere information. How could it

be? They should go to the *Suchdienst* in person, talk to the people there. They should see the documents—if there were any—the pathetic little scraps of paper, the lists, the cards that had been signed and stamped and had dates written on them. They should see, get, if this was the right expression, whatever was the 'next best thing'.

What did they expect, after all, what did they really hope for, these needy and haunted ones who still, after fifteen years, kept coming forward—sometimes mistakenly to his own office—as if their numbers might only ever increase? To be given back the actual ashes, the actual dust, the actual bones?

II

Blushes

Blushes

Dr Cole eased his car from his garage, then stopped to watch, in his rear-view mirror, the garage door slide gently down and the light above it extinguish itself. This had once given him an absurd, vain satisfaction; now it was his only goodbye. The car was expensive and comfortable, as was the house that went with it: large, double-fronted and, like the others in the discreet crescent, enclosed by lawns and leafage.

As he moved off, the purr of the engine and the crackle of gravel were the only sounds, except for—though, inside his car, he couldn't hear it—the great anthem of birds. It was a little after six on an April morning, but at eight it would still be astonishingly quiet. Except for the birds. They had become extraordinarily loud, as if by some conscious effort. But that was an illusion. It was the contrast with the silence. Minutes ago, he'd been lying in bed, listening to them and marvelling. A solitary man in a big house, surrounded by hymning birds.

And the roads, even the main ones, would be empty. They would be just as empty at eight. The phrase 'ghost town' sometimes came to Dr Cole as he made these journeys. Ghost world. He would reach the hospital within fifteen minutes. Normally—when had 'normally' ceased to apply?—it might take forty-five.

As he turned out of the driveway, a fox slipped nonchalantly through the beam of his headlights. One morning, he had counted ten foxes. The birds and the foxes. They had reclaimed the world.

These journeys, on which he also counted foxes, had become his few corridors for thought. Or, rather, for memories that came thick and unbidden—ghosts themselves. He had proved what was commonly said: that when we are old, it is our earliest memories that return to us most insistently. All the later stuff recedes.

Or can be swiftly condensed. Two marriages, one divorce, no children from either marriage; and the second marriage much longer and more meaningful than the first. His second wife had been the love of his life. He could say that without hesitation. But she'd been dead now for most of two years. The loss of his life. She'd died only a year after he retired. For a while they'd lain together in the bed in which he'd just been lying alone, listening, as dawn broke, to the birds. She'd said to him once, 'We can do this now.' As if lying there together were the simplest but greatest gift retirement could bring. It was.

Despite or because of the empty roads, he'd begun to leave earlier than was needed, so that he could deliberately dawdle, even take detours, to permit the gush of memory to run its course. It was memory, not thought. His mind simply filled and throbbed, a function of driving. He vaguely rejoiced in the peaceful roads that allowed it to happen. 'Peace.' That word came to him, too. In a little while he would enter a scene of war.

He had put himself forward. How could he not? He was seventy-two and retired, but how could he not? He was a specialist in respiratory disease. He had retired shortly after his mother had died. She was ninety-two. Decades ago, after his parents' divorce, it was his mother who'd wanted him to be a doctor. It was his mother who'd almost exclusively claimed him, and he hadn't resisted. He had become not just a doctor but, as it proved, a top man in his field. He had fulfilled his mother's dream, and more.

A top man in medicine, but he hadn't been able to save her. Or his wife. Within two years they were both gone. The women of his life.

He had come forward. It was hardly a choice. He'd presented himself like a called-up reservist. They'd been 'honoured' to have him back. Though what did that mean, amid such havoc? A queue of casualties. A queue of deaths. One of which, he clearly understood, might be his own. All of them understood it. It might be any one of them.

What they didn't know, as he strove to be a figure of cool authority, was that he actually welcomed it. It 'took the mind off', as they say. It gave him something to *do*.

And these morning journeys took the mind off in a different way. It didn't happen on his journeys home. He did his extendable, unquantifiable 'shift'. He grabbed something tolerable to eat. He drove home, numb. He slept, in his absurdly roomy home. Thank goodness, he could sleep. It was only on these dawn rides that his life returned to him, from its uncanny distances. Otherwise, it had departed; it had seemed already over. And now he understood—accepted—that it soon might be truly over.

*

34

As he held the wheel, he was a child again. If it were a matter of calculation, he could say with exactness that he was ten. But he didn't have to calculate. He *was* ten.

He was ten, and he was lying in bed on a sunny June morning because he was ill. He saw his mother's face as she leaned towards him. She was sitting on the end of his bed, now and then stroking his covered foot or knee, and, though he was ill, her face didn't look in the least troubled. It looked full of gladness, even quite merry.

She would have been—what?—a woman in her early thirties. And Dr Henderson's face—Dr Henderson!—though it was the face of a doctor and provisionally grave, also looked quite merry. It always happened when he visited. Doctors 'visited' in those days. He would loom in the doorway, holding his doctor's bag, a forbidding figure, more often than not still in his dark winter coat and bringing with him a residue of chilly air. But very quickly he would melt and become friendly, even jolly. And how old would he have been? In his late thirties. A 'young doctor'.

Now he would be dead, of course.

But on this June morning Dr Henderson wore a pale-grey lightweight summer suit. He sat down at the bedside on the chair that was always provided for him. It wasn't part of the bedroom furniture. His mother would fetch it.

The chair for Dr Henderson! He could see it now. It had striped upholstery, red on cream, and he later learned that the stripes were called 'Regency' stripes. Its usual place was in his parents' room, where it seemed not to be used for sitting on, since, when he looked, it was nearly always draped with items of his parents' clothing. So now Dr Henderson sat where his parents' clothes had mingled.

But even before he sat, even as he crossed the room, he said cheerfully, 'Well, Jimmy, you're a lucky man. You might have been poorly on your tenth birthday. Many happy returns, if I'm not too late. Your mother tells me you had a wonderful birthday party. Let's take a look at you.'

He sat on his Regency chair. His mother sat on the bed. This was how it always was. There was no question of its being the other way round. His mother stroked his foot or knee and sometimes leaned towards him. And Dr Henderson bent over him in his professional way.

Each time—each time Dr Henderson called—he'd have the thought, lying there, being 'the patient', that they were like a little family. They were like the little group of three that normally lived in the house. And suppose his father, who was now busy at work, were to be suddenly replaced by Dr Henderson. Would it be so terrible? Dr Henderson even had a way—though at ten he didn't yet have the word—of being 'fatherly'. Was Dr Henderson even more fatherly than his own father?

His mother's face was bright and glad, and there seemed, this morning, to flutter round them all a particular kind of glee. He knew what it was. He felt it himself, and even felt rather proud, despite being unwell. It seemed that he had now completed the important list of illnesses that, though they were illnesses, it was highly desirable he should have. It was like a duty, a duty that had taken, in his case, ten years. His whole life! Each illness was challenging, one or two were nasty, but at the same time they were a source of achievement. Now he had done them all. He was to be congratulated, and not just for his recent birthday.

As he lay there, undeniably ill and the object of his mother's and Dr Henderson's attention, he felt a surge of happiness. Even the word 'happy' seemed to hover over him, like Dr Henderson's not yet conferred diagnosis, like something that might hover over him all his life.

'Well, Jimmy, I'd say, by the look of you, your mother was quite right. She'll be doing my job next. Mind you, as illnesses go, it's not one of the hardest to spot.'

Dr Henderson gave his mother a quick glance that might have been called cheeky. It was a nice glance. His mother often used the word 'cheeky' (mostly about her son)—'Don't be cheeky.' And now it would have been a particularly appropriate word.

Dr Henderson said, 'Scarlet fever. I'd say so, too.'

Then his mother said, but looking slyly at her sick child, 'Unless he's just blushing.'

Dr Henderson couldn't have known what special meaning this had. If his mother had been given to winking, she might at this point have winked.

Dr Henderson half-snorted and half-laughed. 'So what have you got to blush about, young man? Open wide.'

And how clever of him. To have asked such a question, then taken away the means of answering it. The question floated off into the air as Dr Henderson inspected his tongue and tonsils.

'Scarlet fever, no doubt about it. Let's have a look at your rash.'

As he drove now between rows of tomb-like houses, he remembered his little pyjama top, striped, like the chair, but in softer colours, and about to be medically unbuttoned. And he remembered his rash, the creepy feeling of it, and how, long after it had gone away and he was otherwise well, his skin still felt odd and rough.

And he remembered now, like something he might

recite—he was a doctor, after all—the whole list of those childhood illnesses, with their names that were, themselves, faintly childish and fairy-tale. Measles, mumps, chicken pox, whooping cough . . . All of them to be undergone, then left behind, usually for ever, like little heaps of children's clothes no longer needed, like miniature versions of the clothes on his parents' chair.

Children everywhere went through it. The illnesses had once been perilous and in some cases still were, and could even kill. When he was smaller, there had still been the real frightener: polio. Though that had been simply dealt with, one morning, by a jab in his arm. Frightening enough, but he hadn't cried. And his mother, then too, had looked particularly glad, though it was a different kind of gladness; there was even a wetness in her eye.

It was all over. Polio dealt with. A jab in the arm—not as awful as feared. It meant you could never get it, because you'd had it already, in a manner of speaking. His mother had tried to explain. It was called vaccination.

Another fox. In the half-light, you couldn't make out their faces or the redness of their fur, but they always gave the impression that they were sneering.

His bedroom curtains had been half closed—a ritual of sickness. His mouth was silenced again by the insertion of a thermometer. Dr Henderson, armed by his mother's prior—and correct—suspicion, produced medicines from his bag and gave some words of instruction. Two of the pills were to be taken immediately. He wrote a supplementary prescription. Then he removed the thermometer, looked at it, wiped it carefully, and put it back into a little liquid-filled tube.

'It's a mild case, Jimmy. You hardly have a temperature. I've seen much worse. You'll live. You'll be right as rain in a few days if you do as your mother says. And no school for at least a week.'

You'll live!

'As for blushing, I can't cure that. You'll have to take care of that by yourself.'

He frowned, though in an unserious way, then, snapping shut his bag, got up from his chair and looked at his watch. 'Your mother's promised me a cup of tea.'

Dr Henderson was always offered a cup of tea.

His mother got up, too, and they stood together at his bedside, as if he were their child. Dr Henderson said, 'And no playing with your friends, either. Though it seems you've done that already. A wonderful birthday party. You're lucky you didn't miss it. I'm sorry I missed it myself.'

Then they went downstairs, leaving him with the

sudden, oddly upsetting thought that Dr Henderson might never enter his bedroom again—if this were the last illness. Then with the thought, not so upsetting, but puzzling: Why should Dr Henderson be sorry to have missed his party? Had he been invited?

And then with the giddily returning memory, as he lay in bed, of the party itself, every detail of it. A memory, then, merely a week old. But now, sixty and more years later, it came back to him just as rushingly fresh.

That party! That party that even Dr Henderson had wished to attend! Though why, indeed, should he have been there? Why should he have been standing there, like a special guest, among the gaggle of mums? The mums were the only grown-ups at the party. It was a teatime party. There were no men. All the men were absent at work. All the fathers, and the doctors, too.

But it was true. 'A wonderful party.' Dr Henderson had confirmed it—and he was a doctor. The best of his birthday parties, because, after all, he was ten, a big boy, a double number to his name. And the best party because—but this he knew now and not then—in less than a year's time his parents would start the process of not living together. The world would disintegrate.

*

It wasn't his mother and Dr Henderson, as he might have supposed and even, vaguely, hoped. His mother sometimes went to see Dr Henderson by herself. But this was only to 'see her doctor', in his surgery. 'Women's stuff,' his father had once bafflingly said about these visits, and then shrugged, as if he didn't care.

Putting two and two together, he'd later wondered if this 'stuff' might have had to do with the little brother or sister he'd once been promised. But surely that had all been finished-with long before he was ten. His mother and father had settled for just one. So had he—settled on being the one. Looking back, he'd dared to imagine that his mother's visits might not have been about anything medical at all.

But it had been his father. All the other way round. When his father went to work he sometimes didn't, apparently, just go to work.

Though none of this could have clouded his tenth birthday party, any more than could the illness he would have a week later.

Another fox.

A wonderful party on a gorgeous summer's day, in the garden that lay beneath his bedroom window. If he'd got up from his sick bed and looked through the gap in the curtains, he might have surveyed the scene of his party. But he didn't need to—it was in his head.

And it was in his head now.

The lawn was strewn with his 'guests', his school friends. Only an hour before, they'd all been at school, and the lawn had been just a lawn, quietly basking in the June sun. But a transformation had occurred. The boys, including himself, had been thrust into clean shirts and the girls into party frocks. Then they'd all regathered at his house and taken possession of the lawn.

On the narrow terrace between house and lawn stood a table bearing food and drink. Round it, clustered the mums, in party frocks of their own. Under the table, hidden, though not for long, by an overhanging tablecloth, was everything needed for a succession of party games, and the presents to go with them. Everyone, he had previously and confidentially been told by his mother, was to have presents, but he would have the most and the best.

And so it had all transpired. What was on the table was soon plundered—the tablecloth would eventually need a serious wash—and what was underneath soon fulfilled its purpose. The lawn became strewn not just with children but with torn and crumpled wrapping paper and other debris of the games, not to mention many smeared paper plates and cups, some inadvertently trodden on.

All this joyous litter was a tribute to his mother's toil. How she must have laboured that day, preparing little fancy cakes—and one big one—as well as ice cream, jellies, bottles of lemonade, jugs of lemon and orange squash. In the brief interval between his return from school and the start of it all, he'd watched her set everything out with unpanicking efficiency, a calm smile on her face. How she must have worked—wrapping the presents as well!—and how unflappably and triumphantly she assembled the results of her work.

In the unit, soon, he would inwardly invoke, to assert his necessary poise, his mother's busy serenity before his tenth birthday party.

At the last moment she'd gone up quickly to her bedroom to put on her own party frock. She reappeared in a dress that was a mass of swirling red blooms on white, and in a delicate waft of perfume. Her day dress would have been left on the Regency chair.

Then the front doorbell began to ring.

He saw it all now, as he drove towards what was no party at all: the children in charge of the lawn, the women subserviently but floridly in charge of the table, dispensing food and drink and stepping onto the grass—some in unsuitably high heels—only to deal with the games and the crucial issuing of presents.

The names of some of his small friends came clearly back to him, though he had not thought of them for decades: Bobby Scott, Nigel Wilson, Janet Fletcher, Wendy Simms . . .

There they were on the lawn. Where were they now?

A party for both children and mums—an invisible, wavering line between the two. But there was a moment when the mothers all claimed him. They drew him away from his pride of place on the lawn and took him aside. They said things like, 'You mustn't forget us, Jimmy.' Or, 'Let's have some of you, too.'

It was Mrs Simms who said that: 'Let's have some of you, too.' Whatever it meant. She'd just popped into her mouth, almost whole, one of the little cakes, and as she did so, her eyes had bulged and goggled in just the same way as her daughter's did when, with her smaller mouth, she attempted the same.

Mrs Simms! He saw her again, flicking bits of cake from her lips, then waggling her sticky fingers in the air. Her party dress, like all the others, was flowery—they were in a garden, after all—and had no sleeves and a deep collar. When she brushed her mouth a sizeable crumb had fallen into her neckline and disappeared. Did she know? Had she seen that he saw? But she said, after the finger-waggling thing, 'Let's have some of you, too, Jimmy.' And added, 'Us girls, too.'

So all the mums had become 'girls'. It was confusing.

And then she said, which was even more confusing, 'So come on, Jimmy, you've got to tell us.' Her eyes had swivelled round the crowded lawn. 'You can tell us. Which one do you like best? Which one is your favourite?' Then, as if to correct herself, she said, 'Which party frock?'

More and more confusion. Did she really mean, as he'd momentarily thought, 'Which girl?' Or did she mean 'Which frock?' Or was it one and the same? In order to give an answer did he have to separate the girls from their frocks? Which was a thought. Did he have an answer anyway?

So he said nothing. He struggled, a flurry of confusion. Was Mrs Simms really wanting him to choose her daughter, Wendy, both frock and girl? Then another mum—was it Mrs Scott?—chimed in, 'He's blushing!' Worse and worse.

But his mother quickly and gently said, 'Leave him

alone. Let him be. It's his party.' It wasn't a reproach to the other women; it was just a little firm statement that at once saved him. He felt again now, a seventy-two-year-old man at the wheel of a car, its rescuing touch.

And had he immediately stopped blushing? How could he know? And perhaps no one knew, not even Mrs Simms, that he was blushing not at the choice put to him, but at the thought of that crumb that had dropped down her dress. Where had it gone? And at the thought of all these grown-up party dresses, rustling, pressing and whispering round him, which had been put on in more complicated ways than the girls' ones and, it was at least partly true to say, especially for him.

For a moment he'd been claimed by the women, even made to feel he belonged to them. And been made to understand that they were also girls. And for a moment, too, after his mother's magical intervention, he'd even seemed to see everything through their eyes. Not just the spectacle of the party, of the child-sprinkled lawn—supposedly still guarding his secret choice—but *everything*. Everything all around. Not just this garden and its lawn, but all the adjoining gardens, all with their own lawns and apple trees and trellises and cascades of roses. And the houses that went with them, with their red-tiled roofs and glinting windows, many of them flung open as if to draw delighted breath on this scintillating afternoon.

He let his eyes sweep round, in the way their eyes—he saw—now and then swept dizzily round to take it all in. *Everything.*

The houses, his mother had once said, were roughly the same age as him. They'd been new when his parents moved in, the homes of pioneers. Now they'd become lived-in and established and ten years old, but still had an aura of newness, just like him. Inside the houses were new fridges, new electric kettles, new televisions.

Though not inside or even outside them on this radiant day—but had anyone been thinking of them?—were all the fathers who were working like billyo to pay for the whole fabulous enterprise.

Why should Dr Henderson have been invited?

Here and there among the gardens were massive towering trees, their leaves green-gold in the afternoon light, left over from when, he'd been told, it had once been farmland, hedgerows and fields.

He looked around and could even see how, to the mums, it must look like heaven. Everything that they'd once wished and dreamed of. Heaven. They had achieved it, as they'd achieved their children and watched them grow, as they'd achieved this party—if he didn't see it then, he saw it now—a gleeful homage to it all.

He saw that it was happiness. What else? He gasped, holding the wheel of his car, at the sweet returning breath of it. A seventy-two-year-old man driving between heaven and hell. And gasped to recognise that this was his chosen field. Breath. The breath of life.

And why do we blush? Why are some of us prone to this blazoning of embarrassment, which is itself a cause for further embarrassment? Can you blush from sheer happiness, its touch on your skin? He was acquainted with the workings of the human body, but he knew no more about blushing than, apparently, Dr Henderson had known. It wasn't his field.

It was supposedly a malaise of the young and even innocent. 'Blushing like a girl.' Or boy. Later, you got over it. But he knew that he himself could still go pink-faced for no obvious reason. Perhaps he was blushing now, in his car, to recall the blushes of decades ago. Though did you blush—it was a paradox—if no one could see? And, very soon, he would be concealing himself not just in a face-mask but in layers of cumbersome protective clothing. All to spare his blushes?

Was it the crumb in Mrs Simms' bosom, or the vexing question she had put to him? Was it the prospect that lay behind the question, which had never so invitingly floated before him? That life itself might be a great choosing of *girls*. How delightful. What happiness.

But if it was true, it was over now. The women of his life. And he himself might be near the end, for all the care he took with his protective gear.

Near the end and, so it seemed, near his beginning. Ten. It was what they said happened when you drowned. You saw your whole life pass before you. And it was what the patients did, in the unit, when they reached the end. Effectively, they drowned.

The hospital was now very close. He could see, in the dip of the road, its tall incinerator chimney and the spangle of lit-up windows in the not yet full April daylight. At any moment he might be chased and overtaken by an ambulance, with a quick blast of its siren. One morning, he'd been overtaken by three.

In a few moments he would have to switch off his memory. Apply himself only to what was before him. He would have to turn off his life.

How would this pandemic pan out? No one knew. He

could only do what he could, for several uncountable hours, in a place of great suffering. And risk.

Some of the staff were near to snapping, he could see. Psychiatry was not his field, either, but he could see. They had homes and families to deal with, not just in their memories. They didn't have empty mansions with automatic garage doors.

A cheery colleague had said in one of their brief breaks that this was only a blip. The pandemic was a blip. It was just a great preliminary distraction from the real calamity, that the planet would be uninhabitable, for human beings, within a century. Unless miracles were performed.

He saw again the shimmering ancient trees, watching like sentinels over the gardens. He saw the lawn. His father had mown it specially on the eve of his birthday. His father had departed within the year. He saw the party frocks. He saw that wardrobe of illnesses so gallantly worn by little souls, then happily discarded. He saw Mrs Simms. Her bare shoulders. He saw his mother. And he saw himself lying in bed just a week later, his mother leaning towards him, and Dr Henderson in his chair.

It was because of Dr Henderson, he was sure of it, that his mother had wanted him to become a doctor. The two of them had left his bedroom and gone downstairs for their cups of tea. He could hear only the murmur of their voices. No words. Grown-up conversation. Then Dr Henderson had left.

But he heard again now his mother saying to Dr Henderson in his striped chair, 'Unless he's just blushing,' though with that look meant only for her afflicted son. And so he had known, after Dr Henderson had completed his diagnosis, that it must have been on his tenth birthday, at his wonderful birthday party, that he'd caught scarlet fever.

III

CHOCOLATE

CHOCOLATE

The Skinners' Arms. Outside, a cold dank darkness. But never mind the world out there.

Dermot took a sip. 'I knew a girl once,' he said, 'who worked in chocolate.'

The others exchanged the quickest look.

'Was that when you worked in baloney?' Tommy said.

Dermot said, unequivocally, 'I've never worked in baloney.'

'And where was this now? Where she worked in chocolate,' Michael said.

'It was in the city of York, Micky. Have you ever been there? It's up in the north of the country.'

Tommy said, 'I'd take a guess it's in Yorkshire.'

Dermot ignored Tommy.

'That's what she told me, that she'd worked in chocolate. But I have to admit now, I have to be honest, it wasn't so much what she said, but the thought that she put in my head. The thought of her—why should I have thought it?—covered in chocolate. That's what got me going, if you see what I mean. And I bet that's what you was all thinking too, soon as I said what I said. All dipped in chocolate. That's what you was all thinking.'

None of them spoke. None of them denied it.

Dermot took a sip.

'Come to think of it now, that's how she might have put it herself—I mean, when she was working in chocolate. She might have said, "I'm in chocolate." That's how she might have put it. The way people do when they talk about their line of business. Like you might have said once, Tommy, "I'm in sand and cement."'

Tommy took a sip.

'Either way, it would have been the same. Same picture in my head. All covered in chocolate. And I'd swear to you now that that's the picture she meant me to have, wanted me to have. But all she said was that she'd worked in chocolate. And no lies.'

'And you should know about them,' Tommy said.

'Come now, Tommy. Have I ever told a lie in my life?'

'So how could you tell?' Connor said. 'I mean, that she meant ... That she wanted ... I mean'—Connor glanced at Tommy—'if she existed in the first place.'

'You doubt me too, Conny boy? By the look in her eye. Can't you tell everything by the look in the eye?'

It was a challenge. It meant they all had to look into Dermot's eye, where they all might have seen, in its grey-blueness, the image of a girl coated in chocolate.

The average age of the four of them was approaching three score and ten. Add them all up, and they were nearing three centuries.

'There were two chocolate factories in York,' Dermot said. 'Listen and learn. It was chocolate city. At least it was then. I must be talking about the '70s.'

'The 1870s?' Tommy said.

'There was Terry's and there was Rowntree's. They must have been deadly rivals, it must have been chocolate war. And she'd worked in Rowntree's. She'd done time on Kit Kats.'

'I'm sure she had,' Tommy said. He took a sip. 'And what took you to York? Apart from chocolate business.'

'Have you never eaten a Kit Kat, Tommy? Have you never eaten one of them things? But did I say I was there?'

'No, you didn't,' Tommy said, warily.

'But I was,' Dermot said. 'I very much was.' He took a sip. 'I was very much there all right.'

There was a familiar and irritating glint in Dermot's eye—along with the chocolate-coated girl, if she was still to be seen. They took their sips, peering at each other over the rims of their glasses. What did it matter, a tall story or a true one, now they were all well past it? These sessions at the Skinners' had acquired a certain mellowness. When was the last time there'd been a real barney? When was the last time Tommy had taken a swing at Dermot?

'But you haven't said. What you were doing there,' Tommy said. 'Apart from.'

'Oh the usual business. As it was then. The race-horse business. They do a good meeting at York. A fine track. Just a short walk from the station. Up there on a morning train, back again in the evening. Easy from King's Cross. A day out, a change of scene, make a killing at the same time. The usual race-horse business.'

He took a sip.

'And did you? Make a killing.'

'Well, as you know, Tommy boy, I'm never one to discuss money. So long as you and I can buy each other a drink, I never talk about the stuff. And the truth is I don't honestly remember. Do you remember the bets you placed all that while back? In your case best forgotten anyways, I should think. It was a long time ago, the 1970s. And that's no lie now, is it?'

He looked at them all.

'But you—' Tommy said.

'Ah yes now, Tommy, you're right there. Some things I remember right enough. Aren't we all the same? Memory's a funny thing. What it remembers and it doesn't. And, now I come to think of it, I must have made a killing. Yes, I think I did, I think I must have been pretty flush. But, you see, my point would be that, whether I'd made a killing or not, it wouldn't have mattered, it would have been immaterial. Since I made a killing anyway. If you see what I mean.'

The infuriating gleam in his eye brightened, then was suddenly gone. A frown, a spasm crossed his face. It all had a surprising absence of fraud.

'But that's no way to put it now, is it?' he said. 'Shame upon me. That's no way to talk about it. A killing! It was anything but.'

The gleam returned.

'Anything but, I assure you.'

He took a sip. They all took a sip. A mellowness. A soft

brown light. The pint glasses were down to well below the half.

'You mean,' Michael said, as if there was room for doubt, 'the lady in chocolate?'

'I do indeed, Micky boy,' Dermot said. 'And that's a fine way of putting it, if I may so. You're a better man than me. "The lady in chocolate." Indeed. Excuse me now if I raise my glass—and God help me if I don't ask you *all* to raise your glasses—to the lady in chocolate.'

None of them abstained. They all, obediently, raised their glasses, though none of them went so far as to repeat, in the customary fashion, the words of the toast.

There was cock and bull and there was cock and bull. But they'd seen the expression change in his face. It was the most memorable moment of the evening.

And, outside, it was a wretched evening. November. No apparent rain or drizzle all day, but a great damp breath on everything. A cold glisten everywhere.

There were four of them. One day, it might be three. Three ... Two ... And then? Well, yes, it would have to be Dermot, gabbing away, all to himself, and trying it on, even then.

'So who was she?' It was Connor who said it. Someone had to say it. 'The lady in chocolate.'

'Well, I'll tell you no lies.'

They all gave each other the quick sideways look.

'She was a waitress in a café at York station. Or was it in the hotel now, right next to the station? There was a big grand hotel. But same difference. I might have got away, you see, got away from York altogether, without meeting her. Just me and my winnings. But there she was.

'And true now, I must have had some winnings. Not a killing, but winnings. Now isn't that the better word all round? Winnings. I must have done the clever thing of stopping early, quitting while I was ahead, even getting clean away from the track before I lost the lot on the last race.

'And I must have said to myself, "Dermot boy, what you need before you leave this fair city is a nice cup of tea, a proper cup of tea served nice and proper. Not another pint in a pub. A nice cup of tea. That's not going to use up all your winnings now, is it?" Don't ask me why I thought it, but I did.

'And, by God, it was the right decision, since there she was. Waitress service. Taking my order like a darling and saying didn't I want something to eat with it? And saying, before I could get out an answer, that the chocolate cake was very good, it was the best thing going, fresh that afternoon, just a few slices left.

'So what was I going to say? That I didn't want any chocolate cake? So she says, with a smile on her and her little pad and pencil, "One slice of chocolate cake." Which seemed to be her moment to say as well—was it all a plan now?—that she used to work in chocolate herself. Did she have to say it? No she didn't. But she said it, with a smile on her.

'She was new to the job, the waitressing, but, before, she'd had the job in chocolate. Which was all her way, it stood to reason, of getting chatty with me. Or maybe it was me who was getting chatty, I couldn't say. If we were going to get chatty, after all, we might have talked about my day at the races, it would have stood to reason too, but we talked about chocolate.

'"Who would want to leave a job in chocolate?" I might have said. Maybe I did. She didn't tell me about Rowntree's or Terry's, or Kit Kats. Not then. I didn't get the history of York city. That came later. She kept it sort of hanging. And I'd swear she knew I was having that picture of her all the while, coated in chocolate, and she meant me to have it. Sometimes you can just tell a thing.

'Isn't that true now, boys? Sometimes you can't see a thing for looking. But sometimes you just can.'

None of them spoke. None of them denied it.

'Anyways, she brings me my tea, proper little pot of my own, proper china, little jug of milk, bowl of sugar cubes, tongs, tea-strainer, the whole caboodle. I think it must have been the hotel now, I think it was. And she brings me my slice of chocolate cake. She tells me I was lucky—but didn't I know that?—since it was the last slice, the last slice going. And, as it happened, it was her last half hour too. She was off at six, so if there was anything else I might be wanting.

'She didn't have to say that either, did she? And I don't have to tell you, do I? I don't have to tell you. One thing led to another, so to speak. I never took my train back to London that evening. My day in York turned into a night in York, the fair city of York, and that's the whole story of it.'

He took a sip, a biggish sip. His glass was almost drained. Then he looked around with just the slightest hint of puzzlement.

'I haven't told you all this before now, have I, boys? You better tell me if I have. Don't string me along now. No? I haven't? I really haven't?'

It might have been as put-on as anything. But no, he really hadn't. All these years in the Skinners' Arms, but no, he hadn't. Though they'd all told each other the same things several times and a general consensus had arisen not to draw attention to it.

'No? Really?' he said, but as if he knew he hadn't. And of course he knew. If he knew all the other things he said he knew.

'Well, sometimes life can be very sweet, boys, can't it? Too sweet for the telling even. Maybe I never *should* have told you. Let the cat out of the bag of it. The Kit Kat even.'

The gleam again! But he dipped his head to stare for a moment into his nearly emptied glass.

He looked up.

'But I'll tell you all this. She was a sweet girl, a very sweet girl. One of the sweetest.'

There was a good pause, a decent pause. Then Tommy said, 'Well, I suppose she must have been, if she'd worked in chocolate.'

Someone had to say it. It was Tommy. It was as if Dermot had offered them all the opportunity.

Now it was Dermot's turn to buy the next round. He got up, gathering the four empties in the fingers of one hand with the ease of long practice.

As he went to the bar, the others could no longer see his eyes, let alone see what he was thinking. They couldn't see that he was thinking: Well, now they can say whatever it is they say about me when my back is turned, whatever that is. We all get through life, thank God, by never having to hear that.

He was Dermot Sweeney, from County Cork. A Cork man in York. He'd missed his chance to put that in his little story.

But he'd said it to the chocolate girl, no mistake.

As he'd stood up, it was possible to see outside, above the frosted lower half of the window. It was as if the outside had gone away for a while and might have vanished altogether. But no, it was still there. There was still, without any visible rain, the same general saturation. A Cork man in Kilburn. Everything had an inky sheen. On the strip of pavement, on the kerbstones and gutter, on the surface of the street and the droplet-covered bodywork of parked cars, the reflections from the streetlights shone and shimmered.

From inside looking out, before you had to go back out into it, and with two pints inside you, it all had a way of even looking quite appealing.

IV

BEAUTY

BEAUTY

'Mr Phillips?'

'Yes. Speaking.'

It was seven-thirty on a Sunday morning. He was in his dressing gown. But he'd recognised the voice of his son-in-law, Paul, and appreciated the mock-formality.

'Mr Phillips' was what Paul had studiously called him, when they were first introduced by Helen. Another Sunday, not so many years before. 'Mr Phillips ... Mrs Phillips ...' All very proper and respectful, and he'd liked it. He and Ruth had been wondering when—if—they might meet 'the boy', as they'd both begun to designate him. Now here he was, on the doorstep beside Helen, with the obligatory bunch of flowers for Ruth and his scrupulous 'Mr Phillips'.

He'd liked it, and thought he'd let it run for a while. Wasn't that how potential fathers-in-law were supposed to treat potential sons-in-law? A leg of lamb was roasting in the oven. Let the boy sweat a bit too.

But the boy had turned into Paul. And Helen would turn into Mrs Heywood. And he, Mr Phillips, had turned, quickly enough, into Tom. 'Call me Tom.' He'd seen Helen's face relax. And the boy, appropriately enough, was also a 'pupil' who'd turn into a barrister.

If he'd put him through it, just a little, then in truth he'd been somewhat daunted himself.

Jesus Christ, Helen's going to marry a whizz-kid lawyer.

'Mr Phillips?'

'Yes. Speaking . . .' A calculated pause. He could join in the game. Birds were singing outside. 'Yes—Paul—it's me.'

'You have a granddaughter.'

On a grey February day, almost twenty years later, as his train sped through several English counties, he'd remembered that moment. It seemed like recalling a dream. The phone, his dressing gown, the birds. He'd left Ruth upstairs, still half asleep, or perhaps only pretending to be. For most of twenty-four hours they'd been expecting a call. He'd leapt up. 'I'll go. I'll take it downstairs.'

After speaking to Paul, he'd returned, light-footed, to Ruth, who by then was fully awake, eyes wide, and sitting up as if to receive an audience.

A Sunday morning in May. They were both not yet fifty, mere youngsters themselves.

He'd re-employed the formula of their son-in-law.

'We have a granddaughter.'

Then he'd said, 'And she has a name already. Clare.'

Now he no longer had Ruth and he no longer had a granddaughter. It was unbearable. And from the moment of his getting up this morning he'd been haunted by that long-ago figure: himself, dishevelled but overjoyed, in his dressing gown. As he'd shaved, he'd been wearing the same dark-blue dressing gown. How many dressing gowns did you need in a life?

His train had carried him captively onwards, but this was all his choice. Winter scenery had glided by.

And how long a life can seem. Yet how quickly twenty,

thirty—fifty—years can pass. How quickly one scene can overtake another.

Now he was walking with a woman young and old enough to be his daughter along a covered pathway in a campus university near a provincial city. He'd never been before to either the city or the university, though he'd once been, fifty years ago, at a similar campus university when parts of it were still under confident construction.

He wondered whether to mention it to this woman— she was called Gibbs, Sarah Gibbs—in order to remedy unforthcoming conversation, in order to hide his apprehension and confusion.

It was a difficult walk. Words were failing both of them.

Here he was, when it was too late. Everything was too late. Ruth had died six months before. Of natural causes. Cancer was a natural cause, though 'natural' was an easy word. And six months was nothing, it was still yesterday.

And he'd thought that *that* was cruel?

Could you die of unnatural, inexplicable causes? Yes, now he knew you could.

It had been a consolation—another easy word—that Ruth, at least, had never had to know the loss of their granddaughter. The double cruelty was his alone. Though Clare had known the loss of her grandmother.

Had that even been a *reason*?

They had been close, Ruth and Clare. What's more, it was often noted, from the first moments of Clare's being 'shown' by her parents—he'd thought of that day when Paul had been 'shown' by Helen—that Clare had Ruth's looks. Their closeness was prefigured by resemblance. Clare had her grandmother's eyes, her mouth, her way of tilting her chin; you couldn't deny it. It was all rather wonderful. He had been seeing his wife as a baby.

Might he say something of all this to this woman? 'Clare was very close, you know, to her grandmother. That is, to my wife . . .'

Was that a good tack? Or was it better—or more crass— to say, 'I was at a university myself, you know, just like this one. I studied Modern History . . .'?

And feebly joke, 'Now I'm part of it.'

Why hadn't this woman—Mrs Gibbs, Dr Gibbs?—put on a coat? It was February. She'd said, 'It's no distance.' It was already feeling like half a mile.

*

The resemblance had been unmissable. He might put it differently and say that Clare had been as beautiful as her grandmother. They shared their beauty.

He wished he'd said it when they were both alive. Might he say it now to this woman?

But Clare's grandmother had died. Just when Clare was leaving school, when she'd gained a place at university and was turning eighteen, just when she was deserving of blessings and congratulations—not least from her grandmother—her grandmother had stolen her thunder and died.

A reason? A trigger? If only her grandmother hadn't died.

Well yes. He said it constantly to himself. If only Ruth, his wife Ruth, Clare's grandmother, hadn't died.

And sometimes he even said—unreasonably and harshly: If only Clare hadn't stolen his grief.

Cold gusts blew around the pathway. The canopy above them rattled and tinkled. He was in the coat he'd arrived in. This woman must be suffering, in just her white blouse and black cardigan. She must have thought, back in her office, that it would be somehow unseemly, in the solemn circumstances, to go through the petty business of fetching her coat and putting it on.

He had said—it was common decency—'It's chilly out there. Aren't you going to put on a coat?' He hadn't thought that this visit would involve such niceties.

But no. It was 'no distance'. Or perhaps she'd thought that she should appear penitent. Though was it her fault? He hadn't said it was anyone's fault. He hadn't come here to blame.

Though he hadn't come here, either, to console. Poor woman, she must have been going through it.

A black cardigan, a black skirt. To offer a token touch of the funereal? A black skirt that hugged her hips. Was it for him to notice?

'Mrs Gibbs?'

Another phone call.

'Yes. This is—Mrs Gibbs speaking.'

He hadn't known whether to call her 'Mrs Gibbs' or 'Dr Gibbs' or even, possibly, 'Dean Gibbs'. She was, apparently, a dean.

'This is Mr Phillips.' He might have said, 'Tom Phillips', but didn't. 'I'm Clare Heywood's grandfather. I mean, I was her grandfather.'

'Ah.'

He'd heard the tremor of exasperation.

Yes, he could well imagine the tough time of it this woman had been having. Not only imagine; he knew it, from Helen and Paul. Sarah Gibbs was their 'liaison' with the university. Perhaps she'd thought that after three weeks she'd almost weathered it. Now here was an agitated grandfather.

He'd heard the exhaustion in her voice. But three weeks was nothing. How long did you—could you—give such a thing? He'd been told, many times, well-meaningly, that he'd 'get used' to Ruth's death, or, more subtly, that he'd 'get used to not getting used to it'. Well, six months had passed and he hadn't got used to anything. Six months was nothing.

And how did you ever get used to *this*?

'Mr Phillips—please would you accept my deepest condolences.'

A fair start. It was even said with a sort of gentleness.

Then he said, 'There's something I'd like to discuss.' And he thought he'd heard an intake of breath.

Yes, she might have had enough 'discussion'. Enough fielding, in its various forms, the relentless question 'why?' He'd had to steel himself to make this call—to get put through. Now he sensed a steeliness on her part. Perhaps she was really some horn-rimmed harridan.

'No, I don't mean "discuss". There's something I'd like to *do*.'

Less than a week later, on this grey day, he'd found himself in her office. His 'request' had been granted. Could it be refused? A date had been agreed. He'd taken a train. A taxi from the station. He'd been directed to the appropriate administrative block. He was still steeled, still prepared for some harridan. But—

She was beautiful. He hadn't expected it. He hadn't expected to be confronted with beauty. Yet he'd at once thought: Jesus Christ, she's beautiful. Some inner voice that he thought he'd lost years ago had said it, even in such brazen language.

And he was at once bewildered. Doubly bewildered. He was bewildered anyway. It seemed that he'd entered long ago a permanent state of bewilderment. Life had become bewilderment.

She'd stood up, behind her desk.

'Mr Phillips, I'm Sarah Gibbs.'

Forty-four, forty-five? The same age as Helen, a little older. Might that have helped Helen—in their 'discussions'? Could anything have helped Helen? Or Paul.

Forty-five, forty-six? And, probably, a mother too,

perhaps with a daughter of her own, around Clare's age. Why had he immediately thought: daughter? But, in any case, young and old enough to be his own daughter. And beautiful.

She came forward, extending a hand. A black cardigan over a white blouse. A black skirt. What had she made of his own choice: a suit and tie, visible beneath the unbuttoned coat that he seemed uneager to remove? A stern, let's-get-on-with-it look about him. And yet—could she see it?—he'd been stopped in his tracks.

'Please call me Sarah.'

Had he said, 'I'm Tom'?

Bewilderment. The words 'Mrs Gibbs' or 'Dr Gibbs', let alone 'Dean Gibbs', hadn't gone with the word 'beautiful'. If 'beautiful', in this context, was even a legitimate word. He hadn't found any other woman beautiful since Ruth died. He hadn't thought it possible, permissible. Now it was happening, now of all times.

'Please, Mr Phillips, won't you sit down?'

He hadn't wanted to sit down. Sitting down led to 'discussion', to not getting on with it. But he sat, without taking off his coat. A compromise. She hadn't said, after all, 'Won't you take off your coat?'

When she sat too, at her desk again, he noticed, inside

the collar of her blouse, a single string of pearls. He felt a stab, an unwarranted, but undeniable stab. She might have seen his eyes glisten. A present from a husband, for some special occasion. She belonged still to that world in which husbands gave presents to their wives, a world of pearl necklaces. The world he no longer inhabited.

Now she walked beside him, her hand sometimes seeking her throat, as if to coax from it unobtainable words, or to tell herself that, instead of a pearl necklace, she might at least have worn a scarf.

He'd declined, perhaps too briskly, the inevitable offer of a coffee or tea, but seen the flicker of relief in her face. No sitting around for five minutes, clinking their cups. She too, perhaps, wished to get on with it. Or get it over with.

The face had, yes, its signs of strain, but this didn't stop it having its principal effect. He was actually afraid that if they lingered for any length of time, looking at each other across her desk, she must see in his own face the awkward fact that he was attracted to her.

'Attractive': a better, safer word than 'beautiful'? It was almost neutral. But it wasn't the first word that had come into his head. And what did this—business—between them have to do with safety? It was too late for safety. Though she was apparently a dean, charged not with the academic needs of students, but with their general welfare. Their safety. Hadn't she failed, catastrophically?

But he hadn't come here to blame. Though perhaps she thought he had—sitting there, in his coat, like some impatient inspector.

Did she find him frightening? While he found her beautiful.

The pearls had trembled as she spoke.

'You must realise, Mr Phillips, that Clare's room has now been cleared.'

It was good that she called it 'Clare's room', but there was the little collision of 'Clare' and 'clear'. They were the same word. Had she noticed and regretted it?

And 'cleared' was itself a strange expression. But yes, he'd 'realised'. He'd known from Helen and Paul. It was anyway a reasonable assumption. He hadn't been expecting, after more than three weeks, a room that would be 'just as she left it'. A room full of things. Full of Clare. That would have been unbearable.

'Everything that belonged to her has been—taken by her parents. It's just, I'm afraid, a bare room. We are keeping it empty and locked as a—mark of respect.'

He'd thought, but not said: For how long? Long enough for this visit of his? How long would be appropriate? He'd thought: Poor students who had the rooms on either side, who shared the corridor. Poor student who, one day, whenever the period of respect was over, might get allocated the same room.

He said, 'I understand. But even so.'

Meaning: Even so, I'd still like to go there.

Had she been thinking that at the last minute he'd reconsider? Was she worried that she might not get through this little exercise herself? Might he have to hold her hand?

Was she frightened of him?

'Well then.' She got to her feet again, but paused, her fingertips pressing her desk. 'If you're sure.'

'Quite sure. It's why I'm here.' He tried to smile.

She took from among the things on her desk a set of keys. But, for whatever self-punishing reason, disdained a coat.

And now they were walking along a covered but exposed pathway and she must be frozen, but he couldn't bring himself to offer her his own coat. Part of him, in fact, longed to offer it, to be in circumstances where he might not only offer it, but take the opportunity to nestle it around her.

But these were not those circumstances. He was shivering too, even in his coat. These were circumstances that, in any weather, might have caused shivers.

'No distance'? Hadn't she learned the dimensions of her own university? They walked, along pathways, between buildings and wintry lawns, across paved spaces that seemed to have been recently equipped with brightly coloured, screwed-down metal benches and tables, though the paving itself, he noticed, was blackened and puddled. The buildings, too, which must once have been modern and 'contemporary' had streaks and stains on their brickwork.

And as they walked together he was aware of their togetherness in a way that, though he'd imagined that there might be such a walk, he'd not foreseen he would peculiarly appreciate.

Attracted, attractive. The safer words? He was having *feelings* about her, and it was shocking, shaming, bewildering that he was having such feelings when engaged on such a purpose.

And when anyway, for God's sake, he was *old*.

He'd recognised it, accepted it. He was sixty-eight. He'd not recognised it when Ruth died. He'd been sixty-seven,

Ruth sixty-six. He'd felt then, even with gushes of anger: I'm too young for this, too young. Ruth had certainly been too young. But, after this other terrible thing, he'd become old.

Sixty-eight? That's not old, they might say, not these days, it's nothing. But he recognised it. There are things that age you.

He was an old man, even a ridiculous and grotesque old man, walking beside this woman young enough to be his daughter, and having feelings about her. He was in his suit and tie and coat, but he might as well have still been wearing the dressing gown he'd worn this morning. A permanent flapping old man's dressing gown, the February wind now and then revealing his bare blue old man's knees.

And around him were young people. Of course there were. It was a university. They flitted around like so many ghosts, using the paths, going in and out of buildings, crossing the paved spaces with the playground furniture. Some of them nodded, even smiled at Mrs Gibbs, a little sheepishly he thought. And what on earth did they make of him?

He was an old man among ghostly young people, and must look like a ghost to them. Or perhaps like a man who had seen a ghost. Or was going to see one.

*

They hardly spoke. It was a silencing walk. He felt the onus was on him to gallantly dispel the silence, but he lacked the means. What topic was appropriate? And there was no question of their batting between them the word that yet surely hung over them and that had hung over everything for more than three weeks: Why?

No one had the answer. Clare herself had left no explanation. No note. There was nothing she'd said to any friend—or family member—to be recalled, even with hindsight, as ominous.

Why? It started and at once stopped conversations. But it was the only word that mattered. He'd not pushed it forward in his dreadful conversations—if 'conversations' was even the right word—with Helen and Paul. He wasn't going to thrust at them a word for which, though they must have ceaselessly struggled to find it, they clearly had no answer.

Paul was now an experienced legal counsel, no doubt used to sharply getting to a point, but he was as beyond words as Helen. And as for 'counsel'.

They walked. His heart was thumping at what lay ahead. At the same time his blood was tingling, outrageously, at something else. It was being warmed by this woman—who must be freezing—at his side.

Was it all a monstrous conflation? It was Clare who'd been beautiful, Clare who'd taken after Ruth and been beautiful and young and had so many other things going for her. But who'd deliberately and meticulously over a sufficient period of time stored up some pills and then killed herself in the room that he was about to be shown.

They turned, at last, into one of the residential blocks. This must be the one. They went up two flights of stairs. A corridor. The doors to rooms, perhaps seven or eight on either side. He had the dreamlike illusion that Mrs Gibbs, with her set of keys, was taking him to *his* room, to where it would be his lot to be staying, some strange uncategorisable guest. When she'd unlocked the door and shown him the room, she would hand him the key.

And now they were outside it. 'Clare's room.' It was just a door. There was no special sign, least of all an indelible 'Clare Heywood'. Just a number. 16. Between 15 and 17. She unlocked the door and stepped back, to let him enter first.

A bare rectangular room, quite small. A few fittings. A folding flap of a desk. A window with a view, a pleasant enough view of trees—now all bare too—and sloping lawns. Paths. Another of those paved spaces with the toytown apparatus. Her last view.

But it had happened, of course, at night.

A bed, also bare, just a mattress. A single bed. But he knew, from his own direct, if ancient experience, which he had no wish to invoke in detail, how these single rooms and single beds might become intimately shared.

He stood in the room. It was all impossibly cruel. It was like some neat, comfortable, yet punitive cell. Surely not a condemned one.

Why?

Mrs Gibbs said, behind him, 'Would you like, per-haps—some time to yourself? Would you like me to wait along the corridor?'

'No. It's all right.'

He was glad of her hovering presence. And, even now, of—the tingle. Did she feel it? Was it, conceivably, a mutual thing? He felt in any case that she, too, preferred not to be left alone—standing at the end of the corridor, clasping her arms around herself and wondering how long he might need.

While she stood at his shoulder, he scanned the room. Was there, in a corner, some clue, an overlooked clue, some hint that only a grandfather might discern? But it didn't take long to take in everything—and nothing.

It was all he could do, all he could have done. It didn't

even look like 'her', or anyone's, room. He'd never come here when she and all her things had been in it. He'd never visited, proudly, when she was a new university student, eighteen years old, with her life before her. She'd been born—that Sunday-morning call had come—in the momentous year, 2000. What did they think, those flitting ghosts, about their future? He, her grandfather, had been born in the not unresonant year, 1950. And had outlived his granddaughter.

Would it have made any difference if he'd visited? Surely it would have been the last thing she'd have wanted, a *grandfather* turning up to embarrass her before her new-found friends. And in any case, her *bereaved* grandfather, with his smell of age and grief.

But he was here now, with his even stronger smell, the bare trees outside peering in at him like so many assembled witnesses.

After a while he turned and said, 'Okay, that's enough.'

Mrs Gibbs was standing closer than he'd thought.

He said, 'I'm glad I came.' A clumsy statement. But, truly, he was. Even if 'glad' was a preposterous word.

She let him out, then relocked the door. It was as though he'd said, 'No, I won't take it, I won't take this room.'

He thought that she might have been prepared for him to have some kind of convulsion, to weep. Prepared even, to put an arm around him. But no, it hadn't been needed. At least he'd spared her that, and sacrificed, for himself, the chance to receive from her some faltering, pitying—soft, womanly—embrace.

If Clare had been a ghost, haunting her room, what would she have thought to behold such a thing?

Around them again, as they walked back, flitted all those other ghosts. And as they walked back, they walked, once more, mostly in silence. But this time he said it. It seemed it would have been heartless not to. 'It's really freezing. Won't you have my coat?' And—for whatever reason—she declined, with a little determined shake of her head. 'It's all right.' Though she'd clearly been trembling.

He thought, then, that *she* might burst into tears. That she might be the one, in her role of dean, of guardian, of faintly maternal protectress, to suddenly break down. And require comforting.

And, again, as they walked, what small talk was there? Oh yes, I was at university myself once. It was where I met my wife . . .

*

In her office, as he made his final departure and they shook hands, he said once more, 'I'm glad I came. Thank you, Mrs Gibbs. Thank you very much for your trouble.' But he didn't, even at this point, call her 'Sarah' or give her hand some extra affectionate squeeze.

And the strange thing was that even as she'd relocked that door, even as he'd offered her his coat, his extraordinary rush of feeling for her—his attraction, his perplexity before her beauty—began to fade. It seemed itself like some departing ghost.

Was she beautiful? Or had he in some unaccountable way gifted beauty upon her?

When he said goodbye, he said something else. He said that his daughter and son-in-law, Helen and Paul, Clare's parents, didn't know about this visit of his, he'd not mentioned it to them. And he asked Mrs Gibbs if—were she to have any further dealings with Helen and Paul—she might not mention it either. He asked if they might keep this visit of his 'between themselves'.

And that's just what it had been—more than he'd supposed. Between themselves.

She had blinked a bit. Out of surprise, or out of a sense of complicity. Or she'd just blinked. And yes, when she'd blinked he'd thought that her dark-brown eyes were beautiful.

She said, 'I won't say anything.' But she didn't ask why. She just said, 'I understand.'

'I understand.' The words, too, were like a ghost. Nobody understood anything.

On his train back he wondered if Mrs Gibbs would remember him: the man, the grandfather—Mr Phillips—who came to look at just an empty room. Or was she already forgetting him, putting him away, with relief perhaps, in some file for unclassifiable items?

Outside his window, the February sky darkened. The scudding fields and trees became obscure, till he could see nothing of them beyond his own reflection seemingly keeping him company in the dark.

V

Zoo

Zoo

There are certain things that happen in the world, certain big events that make everyone ask afterwards: Where were you when ...? What were you doing when ...? What were you doing when Kennedy was shot? Where were you when the Japanese attacked Pearl Harbor?

Well, to that second question I can answer: Easy, I wasn't around, not by a long way. But I know where my grandparents, Carlos and Teresa, were. They were in Manila. What were they doing? I can't say. Perhaps they were doing what my Grandpa Carlos called 'jiggy-jiggy'. That's what he called it when I asked him once, when I was small, how babies got made. I don't know why I thought my Grandpa

Carlos might best be able to tell me. But he said, without thinking about it for very long, 'Well, little Lucy, grown-up people—a man and a woman—they have to do jiggy-jiggy.'

The next question was obvious: 'What's jiggy-jiggy?' Grandpa Carlos said, 'Perhaps you should ask your mother.' Then he gave me a wink. He made me feel that jiggy-jiggy must be a nice thing. Or perhaps he was winking at the awkward spot he'd now got his daughter, my mother, into.

But Grandpa Carlos liked to give me a wink about lots of things, sometimes for no reason at all. He had a face that would now and then twitch. It would just twitch. So perhaps his winks were sometimes just twitches. He had a face that could make people think that he was Chinese. He once pretended that he ran a restaurant in Gerrard Street.

I can't remember now if I ever *did* ask my mother. Perhaps not. But after Grandpa Carlos's funeral, not so long ago, in Swiss Cottage, I told my Grandma Teresa about how he'd told me about 'jiggy-jiggy'—that he'd used that word when I couldn't have been more than six. And this made my grandma laugh—after her husband's funeral. We'd all gone to her place, though it still felt like 'their place', for tea and cakes. My grandparents loved their cakes.

My grandma, who's gone now too, said, 'Well, Lucy,' (I

was no longer 'little Lucy'), 'I think he might have learned that expression from all the whores in Manila. They used to call out to the GIs, "You want jiggy-jiggy?"' Then she said, 'That was before Pearl Harbor. Now don't ask me anything more.' As if I'd suddenly become 'little Lucy' again.

It was the only time I ever heard my Grandma Teresa mention specifically any of the big events of history, or that I saw, quite clearly in her eyes, almost breaking their surface, the knowledge of terrible things that I must, still, never ask about. All my life, I'd never asked. Though by then I was a grown-up woman in my thirties and, once when I was small, I'd asked my Grandpa Carlos how babies got made.

But I'd made her laugh.

'Have some more walnut cake, darling.'

And I like to think that when the Japanese attacked Pearl Harbor my Grandpa Carlos and my Grandma Teresa were doing jiggy-jiggy—while they still, as it were, had the chance. It would have meant that they were at least getting in practice for making my mother, Carmen. Though that would prove to take a long time, since when the news got through, about Pearl Harbor, they must have thought: Well, now life is *really* going to change for us. It might be going to change very badly, so badly that it might not be a good idea to be even thinking of making any babies. The world's not going to be a good place to bring them into.

And they would have been right. Very right. There was a great deal that my Grandpa Carlos and my Grandma Teresa never told me. Or told my mother. Or, if they told my mother, that she never passed on to me. There was a great deal that would have made it very sensible indeed not to be even thinking of making babies. Though when my Grandpa Carlos told me about jiggy-jiggy, he didn't say that when you did it, you had to be thinking, necessarily, of making any babies at all.

My mother, Carmen, wasn't born till 1944, when it still wasn't a good idea, even less of a good idea, to be having babies. So I think she was an error. Another mouth to feed when, so I've come to understand, thousands of people were starving to death. Error or not, she survived, as did my grandparents. I think that may be the best and rather miraculous description: they survived.

And my mother didn't waste any time in having a first baby of her own. I don't think she was very interested in the lessons of history. And by then—how the world can change—she was living in London, the Beatles were singing 'Please Please Me' and, so I understand too, there was quite a lot of jiggy-jiggy. I think I was another 'error'.

So, as for the other question—where was I, what was I doing when Kennedy was shot?—that's easy too. It was 22nd November 1963. It was my birthday, my actual birthday. I didn't know about Kennedy being shot in Dallas, because I was busy being born in London. My mother was busy too. I was brought into the world on the day that JFK was killed. Does that mean anything? Has it in any way influenced my life? Who knows? But for my two examples of big events that have happened in 'the world', I seem to have picked out two catastrophes that were particularly American.

Not to mention the surrender of the Philippines.

And now I'm getting on for forty. A tricky time, possibly even a too-late time, for a woman, in the baby-making department. But I've had my babies. Two. Andy and Jane. Neither of them errors. So, yes, I know all about jiggy-jiggy. And my babies are old enough now to be doing jiggy-jiggy themselves, even to be having babies. They've never asked me any awkward questions about how they get made. Times have changed again.

But though my babies are grown-up, I can still think of them as just babies. They wouldn't like to know this. I can still think of wrapping them in blankets. Because the world doesn't get any safer. Clearly. And though I've been, myself, through the process of motherhood and I'm getting on for forty, the maternal instinct remains strong in me, just as strong, perhaps, as when I was actually having babies.

That's why when Mrs Olson asked me suddenly if I wouldn't mind looking after Danny for a while, if I wouldn't mind taking him out somewhere, it was such a nice day, I said, 'Of course, Mrs Olson. No problem.'

But now I won't be seeing Danny again. I've seen the last of all three of them. It was the end of Mr Olson's posting, and they've gone. What timing! Though who could have known? And how did Mr Olson get his posting in the first place? London, for a year. So early in his career. If you ask me, there were 'connections' at work, strings pulled. In Washington.

And where's he going to get sent *now*?

In any case, that poor kid, Danny, was never going to know where *he* belonged in the world, except to be carted round it, like a piece of (very expensive) luggage, with them. I think that, after a whole year, he'd just been starting to realise it. A year's a long time if you're only six. They were getting ready to go back home. Meanwhile, he'd been turning into quite a little English boy.

*

'Of course, Mrs Olson. No problem.'

Though I'm not his mother, I'm not a nanny. That's a whole other arrangement.

'You're an angel, Lucy.'

I'm just the maid. At Number 8.

She's already getting ready to go out. She's been on the phone for most of the morning. As she talks to me, she looks at herself in the big gilt-framed mirror, running a fingertip over an eyebrow, patting her hair. She's decided to get her hair done, though her hair looks fine. Then to meet a friend—Kitty Boyd—at the Grosvenor, for a drink and a bite. A 'farewell drink'. The day's already turning into a whirl.

Danny stands beside me as if his mother might be talking to him through me.

Mrs Olson, Nancy Olson, I've learned by now, is an impetuous woman. Not the best woman (in my opinion) to be a junior diplomat's wife. She's apt to tell me, and her son, what she intends to do only moments before she does it. But today is a special day, I grant her. It's not like any day (and neither of us yet knew the half). They have only three days to go, and this evening her husband is getting a leaving party. She doesn't need to get her hair done, or to meet a friend for lunch and so leave her boy in the lurch, in my hands. But why not? She's free to do all these things.

And, looking back now, I can say that, yes, she should have made the most of it, made a whirl of it, while she could.

Kitty Boyd? I know her. I don't mean I *know* her, of course not. I mean I know who she is. One of the Embassy wives, one of the longer-term ones, the taking-under-the-wing ones. They'll be seeing each other at the party anyway, but they've fixed up a separate one-to-one. Why not? And why not get your hair done, into the bargain? A last hair-do in London.

'No problem, Mrs Olson.'

Mrs Olson is in a whirly mood and while she looks at herself in the mirror, I look at Danny, and he gives me a wink. It's a very quick wink, just a flicker of the eyelid, only meant for me. But the wink means something like: My parents are complete airheads, aren't they? The wink is anyway quite a happy wink. And I wink quickly back.

I'm not always sure what my winks at Danny mean, but in this case my wink means: Well, come on then, Danny, let's go and make the most of it. Before you're gone and we won't see each other again. Before I start to miss you.

Which I already do.

Some while ago, he started to call me—never when his parents could hear—'Auntie Lucy'. And he'd say it with an English voice, in a crafty English way. Yes, he's always going to have inside him, even when he's getting on for forty like me, a little English boy. *His* first posting too. It will stick. Not just a little English boy, a little Londoner, with some of the lingo. 'Gissus a kiss.'

And he started to give me those secret winks, and so to remind me, just a bit (though I never told him), of my Grandpa Carlos. Though he was Filipino, but spoke English. I *am* English. The world! What a mix-up. And Danny wasn't a grandpa, he was only six. It was the other way round. It was for Danny to ask me, his Auntie Lucy—if he felt like it—how babies got made. But perhaps, though he's only six, he doesn't need to.

In fact, I'm pretty sure, now, he doesn't need to.

I'm just the maid—the 'Filipina maid'. But I'm English, like my parents. I can't help it if I have some of my grandparents' looks. And I'm not any ordinary sort of maid. I've been the maid at Number 8 for most of ten years. They call it sometimes 'Number 8', sometimes 'The Crescent'. It's just one of their places for staff above a certain level. I wouldn't have said that Mr Olson—Todd Olson—was above that level. Just a new kid on the block. But there we are: connections, strings. He must have swung it. Someone, in Washington, must have swung it for him.

And he must have said one day, over a year ago now, to his all-ears wife, 'And we'll get a house overlooking Regent's Park.' And might have added, 'With a maid.'

And maybe, after that bit of news, the two of them did some quick jiggy-jiggy—if little Danny wasn't in the way.

London! At his level. So: a blue-eyed boy. And Number 8. With the cream stucco and the portico and the railings. Not a palace, but a fine house. And 'overlooking' would be a stretch. Of the neck. They were lucky to get it.

And I was lucky, too, to 'get' it. I know it inside-out by now. Sometimes, though I never say this to anyone, I think that it belongs to me. I belong in it, and it belongs to me.

But it actually belongs to the American Embassy. (And where I actually live, with just Rick now and no longer the kids, is Camden.) I'm not an ordinary maid. I get paid much more than an ordinary maid, and I get paid by the US Embassy, in English pounds. And though I do a maid's work, I have to do it with an extra degree of responsibility, discretion. And I have to do certain, not always specified, things that are beyond a normal maid's work.

Though they shouldn't include being a child-minder. That's a separate set-up.

Usually, though I've never said this to the Olsons, the ones I 'look after', the ones who qualify for Number 8, are of the senior, silver-haired kind. No small kids in tow. And what are *wives* for? What are Embassy wives for? To be shopping at Harrods and getting their hair done all the time? No, Mrs Olson—*you* go and take little Danny to see the changing of the guard.

Nonetheless: more than just a maid. Part maid, part care-taker. Part everything. You have to show them the ropes. And, of course, you have to speak perfect, fluent, educated English. Which I do. Of course I bloody do. I'm not a 'Filipina maid'.

Though when I got the job, all those years ago, things were different. I already had plenty of general maid's experience and good references, but I had to be vetted. Not just interviewed, vetted. And I played the 'Filipino' card then. You bet. I said that my grandparents were Filipino. Real Filipino. But that they'd always worshipped America. I think I might actually have said 'worshipped'. Because America had saved them. They were there, you see, when the Japs arrived. And they were still there—or just about still there—when the Americans came back to kick the Japs out. Oh yes, they could remember General MacArthur. With his corn-cob pipe. Keeping his promise. My grandparents had always loved and been for ever grateful to America. They'd wanted to *go* to America. But they only got as far as England.

So here I am—English myself—wishing to be of service to the American Embassy.

I played the Filipino card. And most of it true. Though you could say that in order to 'save' my grandparents, the Americans had abandoned them in the first place, for three years. And I never said—but my Grandma Teresa hadn't told me yet—that my grandpa could remember all the prostitutes calling out to the GIs.

And maybe it swung it. It got me the job and the money. And maybe little Danny swung it for Mr and Mrs Olson, without ever knowing it. Maybe Mrs Olson had said to her husband, 'Well, Danny's going to need a proper bedroom of his own, isn't he? They can't just give us some *apartment*.' So—with whatever other string-pulling—they got the house. They got Number 8. And they got me.

But the world? That's not my job. I look after the house, so they can look after the world.

*

'No trouble, Mrs Olson.'

It was September. The sun was shining brightly over Regent's Park. In three days' time they were going back to Washington. But, first, Mr Olson was getting a leaving party, a send-off. If he was getting a leaving party, then he couldn't have messed it up, he must have earned his spurs. A leaving party and a sort of launch party—for his future career. And Mrs Olson was making a day of it.

'That's fine, Mrs Olson. I have a feeling Danny might like one last visit to the zoo.'

I was looking at Mrs Olson now, so I couldn't give Danny any more winks.

'The zoo! Well, yes of course. What a great idea. Why didn't I think of it?'

A good question. Why didn't she? Danny's attachment to the zoo, just minutes away, was by now very established. He was going to miss it. He was too young to go there by himself, close as it was. So guess who mainly took him.

But I didn't say anything. I could sense Danny's unspoken 'Thank you, Auntie Lucy'. He didn't quite— in front of his mother—squeeze my hand. I gave a little cough. A practised, patient maid's cough.

Mrs Olson said, 'Oh—yes, of course, Lucy.'

She fetched her handbag and fished out some notes. She was well used to English money by now, but not to the price of everything. Her eyes showed it. Two tickets to the zoo, one adult, one child.

'Oh, and you must get him something for lunch. And an ice cream or something.'

Plus one, two sandwiches. Plus one, two ice creams.

'That's plenty, Mrs Olson. I'll bring back any change.'

She waved her hand. She looked at her watch.

'So—I'll be off. I'll grab a cab. I should be back by three.' Then, as if she'd almost forgotten her son, or his total compliance was assumed, she said, 'Be good, won't you, Danny? Have fun.'

No little kiss.

She dallied in the hallway for a moment, to put on the black jacket that hung on the stair post. In the hallway were several small English landscapes and, opposite another gilt-framed mirror, a quite large painting of a vast herd of buffalo crossing some western plain. Every item of furniture in the house was on my mental list. I wondered how much the Olsons would remember any of them.

But Danny would remember the zoo. I knew that he would be only too glad of his mother's suddenly busy schedule that made this last visit possible. And only too glad of having his Auntie Lucy to swing it. Otherwise, he might have been forced into the position of pleading at some point directly with his mother: 'Mom—can you take me, one last time, to the zoo?' And got no joy.

It might not have meant much to Mr and Mrs Olson, but it had begun to mean a great deal to Danny. They'd come to London and hadn't known that, just across the road (so to speak), they were going to get lions, tigers, elephants—you name it. And he was going to get his Auntie Lucy to take him, several times, to see them. Lions, tigers, all kinds of animals, including, as it happened, in a drab enclosure and always seeming very displeased with his situation, an American bison.

'He doesn't look very happy, does he, Danny? Do you think he has a name? What shall we call him?'

'Bill.'

What a smart little boy. It became, on every visit, a sort of ritual, to go and see Buffalo Bill and try to cheer him up. And now Danny could say his goodbye to him, since Buffalo Bill wasn't going to be doing any going back.

We're going to live in London, Danny! So they must have announced once. We'll show you all the sights of London! *They* would show him? They hadn't even known that the London Zoo was in Regent's Park, and certainly hadn't known that, of all the sights of London, the zoo would be the one their son would most want to see. And keep on seeing.

Though can you call the London Zoo one of the sights of London? Since it's really the sight of all the animals that come from everywhere *else* in the world, anywhere but London. And this would be the same for any zoo. Wasn't there a zoo in Washington? A zoo is a sort of prison for the rest of the world. Which is not a very nice idea at all.

But a zoo is also—just a zoo. Where you can buy a ticket and go through the turnstiles and see all the amazing animals and even lick an ice cream while you do so.

'Come on, Danny! Get yourself ready.'

How many times, in the course of a year? Once or twice with his parents, perhaps seven or eight (if only to get him off *their* hands) with—his auntie. And, now, one last time. His own 'leaving' party.

I still had maid's work to do around the house. Well, too bad. Mrs Olson seemed not to have considered this. I'd have to catch up later.

It was a little after eleven-thirty. Barely dawn in America. Eastern time. Part of the job: always have in mind what time it is in Washington.

Mrs Olson would soon be sitting, wrapped in some gauzy pink covering, at the hairdresser's while her son and his Auntie Lucy (she had no idea that her son called her that) would be wandering among the cages.

Come on! Let's go and see some animals!

As we left Number 8, he reached out his hand for me to take. When had he first done that? When had it become that way round? One last visit. But let's not get all sad about it, Danny, it's a lovely morning and here we are again. What shall it be? Buffalo Bill, of course, but then what? The lions and tigers? The penguins? The monkeys? The fish? The creepy-crawlies? We can't see it all.

Of course not. Not in one go. Though, in a year, we must have done it all, more or less. So I, his Auntie Lucy, had become quite an expert on what there was to see. And, of course, zoos are supposed to be 'educational'. They—the Embassy—had fixed up for him, since he came, necessarily, with his parents, some elementary (but quite superior) schooling. Though wasn't the principal lesson to be had in the London Zoo?

Well, I hope, Danny, it wasn't too much of a cage for you, your London cage. The first of many. All of them very comfortable, expensive and safe. Safe? I hope I made Number 8 quite a nice cage. Your first one, so the one, perhaps, you'll most remember. And I hope you'll always remember anyway—but I think you will—our 'escapes' to the London Zoo.

We made no particular plan, we followed our feet. Of course, we said hello—and goodbye—to Buffalo Bill. There he was, in his mangy coat, slumped on his folded legs, his huge grumpy horned head looking back at us for a while. Did he recognise us? You couldn't help feel it. Was he thinking: There are those two again? You couldn't help wondering what all the animals were thinking, looking back at the people looking at them. Though a lot of them didn't do any looking back at all.

Have you noticed, Danny, that when the animals look back at us, they all look back with the same look in their eye?

And, perhaps inevitably, we finished up with the monkeys. The monkeys were nearly always active and could be relied on to give good value—to swing and jump about and screech and chatter and generally look as if they were happy to put on a show. The monkeys, on this last visit that must have its touch of sadness, would be most likely to make us laugh.

And then I bought sandwiches—seeing all the animals

getting fed made you hungry too—and, yes, we had ice creams. We sat at a wooden table, licking ice creams, a woman of nearly forty and a boy of six, both of us, perhaps, having the same thought: We might be animals, ourselves, in some enclosure, doing this, being looked at. This is typical behaviour of the human species.

What were you doing when? Where were you when?

Had there been some strange ripple running round the outdoor café, round all the people who'd decided on this day to come to the zoo? Had we noticed something, apart from the antics and sounds of countless animals, starting to create a stir around the zoo?

I must have looked at my watch, and said, 'Well, we best be getting along, Danny.'

He said, 'Gissus a kiss.'

And when we got back, all hell had broken loose. Mrs Olson had returned, her hair immaculate, but her general appearance very much not. The television was on. It was about half past two. And there were pictures, terrible, unbelievable pictures, coming from New York, that were going to be repeated over and over again, as if repeating them would make them less unbelievable. They were being seen, already, all over the world.

In New York, in Washington it would still be half past nine.

Mrs Olson said, 'They've cancelled his party. Just cancelled it! Well—what can they do?' Then she said, 'They had the TV on at the Grosvenor. In the lobby. In the bar. They had the fucking TV on!' And then she said, her eyes not turning from the TV at Number 8, 'What now?' And she kept on saying it. 'What now? . . . What now? . . . What fucking *now*?'

And Danny said, 'Do you want to know what we saw at the zoo?'

Mrs Olson said, 'Todd said he can't come back here. Not now. He has to stay at the Embassy. He said they've gone into some kind of mode. Some kind of *mode*!'

It was as if she'd wanted him to be there—for her. She seemed not to have noticed—not even heard—her son, her little boy, Danny, who might have wanted his mother to be there for him.

'Mrs Olson, did you get any lunch? Can I get you anything?'

'Lunch? Fucking lunch!' Then she said again, 'What now? . . . What now?' And kept on repeating it, like the pictures being repeated on the TV.

Where were you when? I was in a hotel lobby in London,

having just had my hair done. I was looking forward to the evening. I was having a good day, I was looking forward to lots of things. I was looking forward to going back home again to the States.

Yes, the monkeys were quite active. As if they appreciated—but it must always seem like it—all the people who'd come to see them, and they were glad to perform. Two of them were being particularly active. And this was making some of the people laugh and squeal at each other or clamp their hands over their mouths, and behave a bit like monkeys themselves.

In all our visits to the zoo, we'd never witnessed such a thing before, which, if you think about it, was quite surprising. But there it was, happening now, on this last visit.

I wasn't in the least embarrassed, standing beside Danny, holding his hand. Perhaps I was even smiling to myself and thinking of a time, long ago, when I'd been roughly his age.

The question was: Was he going to say something, ask something? Yes, he was.

'What are *they* doing, Auntie Lucy?'

Was it an entirely innocent question, or did he just want to know how I'd manage? Was he having fun with me, as all the people were with the monkeys?

'Well, Danny, they're doing—jiggy-jiggy.'

Did I keep a straight face?

'What's jiggy-jiggy?'

I didn't hang back. I didn't say, 'Ask your mother.' Definitely not. I gave him something to think about, quite an education.

I said, 'It's something animals do, Danny. As you can see. In fact, it's something people—grown-up people—do as well. Because, after all, people are animals too. *We're* all animals too.'

He clutched my hand.

I suppose there would have been monkeys in Manila, and I suppose that, back in those dark days, Grandpa Carlos and Grandma Teresa, if they were lucky enough, might have eaten them.

'Auntie Lucy—is jiggy-jiggy how babies get made? Is it how babies get brought into the world?'

He actually said that. He used the words 'brought into the world'. With his nice English accent. In a few days' time, he knew, he'd have to be American again.

What a smart little boy. How could he have come to ask such a remarkable—and highly relevant—question? And he even answered it himself.

'It's how babies get made, isn't it?'

'Yes, Danny, it is. How did you know?'

'Oh, Auntie—I think I just knew it. I think I just *knew*.'

He might almost have said, 'I wasn't born yesterday.'

VI

HINGES

Hinges

One morning in April their father, Ted Holroyd, suddenly died and a few days afterwards Annie and her older brother Ian, both still a little dazed, went to see the minister who, as Annie put it, was going to 'do' their father's funeral. There was surely some better word than 'do', but Annie couldn't, for the moment, think of it.

'Conduct,' Ian had suggested in his big-brotherly way, though with a touch of tongue-in-cheek. Would that make him a conductor then, Annie thought, not a minister? And she imagined this man they were about to meet turning up at the funeral with a baton or with one of those strap-on machines with which bus conductors used to issue tickets.

Both ideas strangely pleased her, though she didn't share them with Ian. Sitting beside him while he drove, she reached out and touched his shoulder, just a light scuffing with her knuckles. Ian almost flinched.

For Annie, one of the effects of losing her father was that she also lost words. They suddenly went missing. Even the words that did present themselves could seem odd and unreliable. 'Minister', for example, was an odd word.

Their meeting with the minister was itself about words, since its main purpose was to tell the minister things about their father so that the minister, in his address at the funeral, could, in turn, say things about him. This, they both felt, was essentially, as Ian had put it, a 'scam'. The minister had never known their father, and they now had to prime this man, whom they themselves didn't know, so that he could speak about their father as if he'd been a bosom pal. So a better word than 'minister', Annie thought, might be 'imposter'. Obviously, it was *not* a better word. This thing, the funeral of their father, would be a pretence. Yet they had to pretend that it wasn't a pretence. Was there a word for that?

In any case, their meeting with the minister posed a basic difficulty: *what* to tell him about their father? They were already coping with the greatest of difficulties: their father had died. And this difficulty had confronted them with an equally great difficulty, which they hadn't exactly discussed with each other: the consciousness, never so sharp, that they themselves would die, that they themselves were mortal. That they were, as it were, 'next', and one day their own children might go to a minister, in just this way, with a similar purpose and find themselves in similar perplexity.

In the car, she'd reached out and touched Ian's shoulder in the lightest way, yet it had caused his own light touch on the steering wheel—she'd seen it—to tighten. She'd felt the tensed and tingling Ian inside Ian. If it had been the other way round, he would have felt the Annie inside her. She had only gently brushed him with her knuckles, but it had been like touching something invisibly 'live'. A conductor.

She was forty-nine, Ian was fifty-one. They both had families. She was Annie Stevens. She hadn't minded, twenty years ago, changing her name. But now perhaps, it occurred to her, she should think of herself as Annie Holroyd again, and she even felt a slight sense of having committed a twenty-year treachery. Her dead father was the man who'd 'given her away'. What a ridiculous expression. She'd clutched his arm and he'd . . . conducted her up an aisle.

Ian didn't have her difficulty, or theoretical treachery. He was Ian Holroyd and always had been. He had other difficulties—and they were word difficulties, too. He had decided to deliver the eulogy. First-born and son—so who else? 'Eulogy' was another worrying bit of vocabulary. Ian preferred to call it his 'few words'. But what to say? Especially as the minister would be saying something, too.

Poor Ian. And then she'd suddenly declared that she would read a poem. She didn't have to do anything. She could just sit in the front row, if she wanted, a mere spectator, with her mother. But she felt that she should be part of this thing, do her bit. And if both Ian and the minister would be 'speaking', what did that leave?

Ian had no doubt thought: Annie? A *poem*? And might even have thought: She's not going to read some poem of her *own*, is she? Some poem she's specially *written*?

Definitely not. What an idea. Just a poem. People often read poems at funerals. So she'd committed herself.

'Okay, Annie,' Ian had said in the rather clipped way he could sometimes say okay. 'What poem?'

'I'll think about that.'

Their mother, who was present, had said, all too quickly, 'Oh, that'll be nice, Annie, a nice poem.'

Ian had perhaps also been thinking: Well, it's all right for Annie, just reading a poem, not having to say anything of her own.

Their mother had decided not to come with them to meet the minister. Her decision hadn't entirely surprised Annie and Ian. Since their father's death, their mother's basic stance had been to disclaim any active involvement in the situation, as if this thing weren't happening to her, or weren't happening at all, and her position, unhelpful as it was, had to be somehow respected. It was a sort of prerogative. Annie had even begun to think—though she didn't tell Ian this—that there was something to be said for it. It had its own odd integrity.

Almost at the last moment, their mother had said, as if some more interesting opportunity had come up, 'No, I don't think I'll go with you. I'll leave it all up to you, chicks.'

It was clear that there would be no further debate. This was their mother. Her husband had died, and leaving it up to everyone else was her fall-back.

There was a pause. Ian had taken a breath and said, 'Okay, Mum.'

But Annie and Ian had looked at each other. When was

the last time they'd been called 'chicks'? Most of forty years ago. In Kirby Street.

One way or the other, before meeting the minister, they'd not been disposed to like him. Annie had seen that this was unfair. The poor man would only be doing his job and no one else would be 'doing' their father. So she'd said to Ian, 'Let's be nice to him.'

Yet, from the start, she *hadn't* liked him, and being nice to him wasn't so easy. Liking or disliking people was a complicated thing. His name was Shepherd. Well. 'Call me Tim.' He had thin sandy hair, hazy-blue eyes, and an apparently ineradicable smile. He spoke with a voice that was patient, kindly and persuasive. What was not to like about him? But she didn't like him.

Hardly had she entered his presence than Annie found herself thinking of Betty Sykes, the mother of her school friend, Sally Sykes, and a neighbour of theirs in Kirby Street in the days when she and Ian had been their mother's 'chicks'. Betty Sykes! Betty Sykes could spend a great deal of her time, arms firmly folded before her, in her front doorway, leaning on the frame, eyeing the street up and down, ready to give lip. The doorway would have been the one to number 33, across the road and along a bit.

Betty Sykes didn't give a cuss what came out of her mouth—and much of it was cusses—or who listened. As a small girl, Annie had often listened, and, against all the evidence, she had *liked* Betty Sykes. She'd even felt, with a child's strange instinct, that Betty Sykes was a good woman with a warm heart inside her. She possessed some vital spark. Betty Sykes had always had, at any rate, a smile for her, little Annie at number 12.

Then it also came back to Annie, in front of this smiling minister, that her father, Ted Holroyd, now dead, had once said to her mother, Mary Holroyd, after the two of them had been talking, and perhaps not kindly, about Betty Sykes, 'Aye, but all the same—'andsome woman.' And had instantly regretted (young as she was, she'd noticed it) that those words had come out of his mouth.

Kirby Street. Betty Sykes! Sally Sykes! How it all came back. Now here she was meeting this impeccably benign minister and she didn't like him. And she and Ian were here to tell him things about their father.

The minister hadn't seemed too troubled by the absence of their mother. He'd told them, in fact, that, quite often, the widow would not feel 'up to it', and he'd find himself talking, as now, to sons or daughters, or both. His smile seemed undimmable. It was perfectly all right. And he'd meet her anyway 'at the occasion', as he put it. It was strange to hear their mother referred to as 'the widow'.

The minister had first gone through various practical matters that they would need to know about the funeral. He explained that they would have to put together an Order of Service—the little leaflet that would be handed to everyone to refer to. And to keep, if they wished. There was still time for doing this.

With such things, she and Ian needed only to listen and nod. But when it came to the nub of the matter, their father's life and what was to be said about it, they both found themselves bewildered. They hadn't done much 'homework', they hadn't explored it properly between them. Perhaps they'd thought—foolishly—that they might leave it to their mother. Or perhaps they'd thought that it wouldn't be a problem, it would take care of itself. He was their father, wasn't he? Did they need to do homework in order to talk about their own father? The idea was even distasteful.

Ian, in any case, was concerned that the minister should not use up any 'material' that he might need in his eulogy—that there'd be enough 'left over' for him to say. But what *was* this material?

The fact was that, when the moment arrived, they didn't

really know what to tell the minister. They didn't know what to say about their father whom they'd known all their lives. They were curiously at a loss. At a loss. Exactly.

Or was it simply that the 'material' itself was just—well, rather thin? They hadn't dared say this to each other. Their own father, and his material was thin?

He had lived most of his life in the same Yorkshire town. He had spent most of his working life in the same place: Batley's, as in Batley's Blankets. He had worked in blankets. What could you say? Then he'd retired. Sixty-five and just in time, since Batley's had soon retired, too. Or closed down. Then, with unexpected and almost unseemly speed, Ted and Mary Holroyd had flown south, to where their son and their daughter had flown long before, finding jobs, lives, marriages, and children of their own. Suddenly, there they all were, the Holroyds, living in deepest Surrey.

And then, quite quickly again, it had seemed, Ted and Mary had gone into 'sheltered accommodation'. Quite snazzy sheltered accommodation, as it happened, largely paid for—but did the minister need to know this?—by her and Ian. And Ted Holroyd had taken up golf. Who would have thought it, Ted Holroyd playing golf? But it was what retired people did. And what was in it for the minister? 'He played golf.'

Not a good subject, anyway. Since, one morning, in his seventy-sixth year, Ted Holroyd had died of a heart attack at the golf course. No, not actually playing golf, let alone at the eighteenth hole, having completed his best round ever, which would have made a perfect story—and Ian would have wanted to keep it for himself—but still in the car park, pulling out his clubs from the boot of his car.

And that was about it. What more was to be said?

So why did her mind keep rushing back to Kirby Street?

At one point the minister, who'd jotted a few things down in a notebook and said, 'I see . . . I see,' had asked, with his still patient and now coaxing smile, 'I wonder if you could give me—well, a sketch—of the man himself.'

A sketch? What did that mean? Was their father to be turned into a sketch? Annie, who had been slightly coming round to seeing things from the minister's point of view, now found herself bridling. Even becoming, inside, a bit like Betty Sykes. Folding her arms. 'I'll give yer bloody sketch!'

But the uncomfortable truth was that they struggled to give the minister even a sketch of their own father. Or, to put it another way, what they *could* give him seemed only—sketchy.

And poor Ian. What, indeed, was he going to say, if

they couldn't even give the minister enough to be getting on with?

But the minister hadn't seemed too deterred. His default position was undaunted capability. Perhaps he was used to this sort of thing: people coming along to talk to him about their loved ones and then discovering that they had no idea what to say.

He continued to smile.

'And you, Annie, you are going to read a poem. Might I ask—which poem?'

She didn't like his familiar 'Annie', or his 'might I ask'. And she didn't like the question, though she knew that Ian would be as interested as the minister in her reply.

'I haven't chosen yet.'

It was a straight answer, but it sounded shifty. The truth was that she didn't have a clue which poem. Which poem went with her father.

'Well,' the minister said, 'there's still time. I'm sure you'll pick a good one. Nothing too long.'

Then the minister paused and for the first time looked a little tentative. His eyes darted between them.

'One last thing I should mention. When people say things—or just read them—they sometimes . . . they sometimes break down. They don't expect to, but they do. If that should happen—if you find yourself in difficulty—just give me a signal, and I'll take over. You can leave it to me.'

Break down? What did that mean? And if you were in difficulty, how could you give a signal?

'Though I'm sure,' the minister had said, his certainty returning, 'you'll both be fine. It will all be fine.'

Fine? A funeral?

Now the thing itself, the 'occasion', had begun. And, yes, she had chosen a poem. And Ian must have prepared his eulogy, though he hadn't disclosed what he would say, and she'd felt she shouldn't press him. His 'few words' might be just that. And it had to be hoped that the minister wouldn't pre-empt any of them.

And now the minister was standing at a lectern, about to give his address, his calm and calming smile directed this way and that, to include them all. But he was leaving a careful pause before he spoke, so that they could settle and adjust. A coffin had been placed before them, like a special exhibit, and it was the minister's task to shed light on this situation.

Outside, moments ago, in quite cheerful April sunshine, their mother—who could not deny any more, try as she might, that this thing was happening and that she had a central part in it—had met the minister for the first time. His consoling and unavoidable arm had been extended towards her. This was the man who was going to 'do' her husband. Annie guessed that the inadequate yet useful word 'do' must be rattling inside her mother's head, too.

The minister's strange white robe had billowed in the breeze. Puddles had gleamed. Car windscreens had shone. There was a vague atmosphere of freshness and merriment, reminiscent of a wedding. Not so far away, a hearse had waited, discreetly yet visibly, with its cargo of something strewn with flowers, for its moment to creep round and pull up.

Then it was doing just that, and Annie, beside her mother, both of them wearing little black hats, was suddenly not forty-nine years old and standing at the entrance to—what was the right word, a 'chapel', a 'crematorium'?—but nine years old and standing in a simple doorway with, not her mother but her father, the man who was in the hearse, under the flowers, in the coffin.

It was not the middle of a cemetery in Surrey, which on this April morning looked particularly green and spring-cleaned and even brought to mind the inappropriate words 'sheltered accommodation', but Kirby Street. Number 12,

Kirby Street, to be precise. Nearby, though not quite within view, there was open moorland. Not nice moorland, with heather and glinting rocks, just dirty-brown moorland.

But it was a nice sunny morning, a Saturday, and she was nine years old, perhaps ten, and was waiting with her father, Ted Holroyd, for another kind of vehicle to pull up. A carpenter's van.

Her mother was somewhere inside the house. She seemed uninterested in the arrival of the van. Ian must have been playing Saturday-morning football.

Her father had said, 'Don't you worry, Annie, it will all be fine. Joe will put it right, just you see.' So the carpenter's name was Joe. And her father seemed to know him.

The front door was open, and the door was the matter at hand. It was painted black and, with its knocker and letter box, was, except for its number '12', like all the other front doors in the street. But it had recently developed an unfortunate creak, even a groan, like an ailing person, and she, Annie Holroyd, had developed a curious pity for its suffering. This was absurd. It was only a door, an inanimate object, but it was a very important object, the door to their house.

Her father had noted her peculiar anxiety. This was why they were waiting for the man who might bring a cure.

Her father had applied bike oil to a suspect hinge, but

this hadn't silenced the door for more than a day or so. Finally, because its moans were no longer to be endured, or because of his daughter's strange concern, he had arranged for a carpenter to come. But he'd made his daughter's concern only more concerning by explaining, as they stood there, waiting, that the door must be ninety years old.

'All these houses, Annie, all the houses in Kirby Street, are ninety years old. Just think of that. Queen Victoria were on throne.'

If the door was ninety years old, then no wonder it was groaning. Had she understood, small child as she was, the magnitude of ninety years, or reflected that the door might be ten times as old as she was? And who was Queen Victoria?

But she surely couldn't have thought, then, what her forty-nine-year-old self could think: that ninety years was the length of a decent human life, though rather longer, as it had proved, than her father's. And she surely couldn't have thought then, as she thought now, that there were two things, generally made of wood, specifically designed to accommodate the dimensions of a single human being. Two objects of carpentry. A door and a coffin. It was like the answer to a riddle.

*

The hearse had come round and stopped. There was another moment of almost-gaiety. Some people took photos of the hearse. It was still possible, somehow, to chat, to make light-hearted remarks. Yet at the same time she was *there*, with her living father, in the doorway of number 12. It was not a matter of seeing it, as it were, from a distance: she was *there*. Since she was only nine or ten, the doorway, in this case, was able to accommodate two.

They were waiting, rather stupidly, like a reception committee, for a carpenter. And that's just what the carpenter had said when he arrived: 'What's this then—reception committee?' She had no idea what those words meant, but they seemed to have caused a grin. Her father had said, 'Hello, Joe.' On the carpenter's van it said 'J. Short'. Even though she was only nine or ten, she could put two and two together. He was Joe Short.

As in 'life is short'. Who had said that? No one. She was thinking it only now, forty years later—it was a grown-up thing to think. But perhaps Joe Short had exuded the words in his very being—to be true to, to live up to his name. Life is short, so grab it quick.

He had, at any rate, a way, a quick look about him, a quick smile. He wasn't short—he was as tall as her father. He was a workman and he was here to do a job of work, but a ripple, a current of something that wasn't work seemed to run through him. He had a look. If she'd been a good deal older, she might have said to herself, ''Andsome man.'

Only nine or ten, but she'd fancied him! The first time she'd appreciated a handsome man—other than, of course, her father.

For some reason, she'd clutched her father's hand.

Now, as they all sat, looking at the coffin and waiting for the minister to speak, she took her mother's hand. She sat on her mother's left, Ian on her right. She had resolved in advance that when this thing began she would take her mother's hand—if her mother hadn't already taken hers—but that she wouldn't at this stage give it any particular squeezing. It was for her mother to do any squeezing first.

In fact, her mother's hand felt inert. She had merely picked it up. She couldn't tell if any hand-holding was going on with Ian on the other side. To know that, she'd have to peer very awkwardly round her mother, who was staring rigidly ahead at the coffin, unaware, so it seemed, that she had a hand.

Her mother's fingers felt weightless and untrained, like a child's. It was as though she, the daughter, were the mother and her mother an infant. But, then again, she herself had become a nine-year-old child, gripping her father's hand. And it was surely more important, in this immediate situation, to have the feeling of holding her father's hand than that of holding her mother's.

When she'd taken her mother's hand she, too, had been looking straight ahead at the coffin, so she hadn't 'taken' her mother's hand so much as 'found' it. That was the expression: she'd found it. She'd found her father's hand in the same way, because she'd been looking at Joe Short. Now she was looking at her father's coffin. It wasn't 'her father's coffin', she'd been telling herself. It wasn't an empty box. Her father was in it. Everything was getting very jumbled up.

Now the minister had started to speak. His warm gaze held them all, and he began to talk with authority and confidence about a man he had never known. In the hushed space, his voice rang out and everyone was listening intently, yet none of it rang true. None of it had to do with the man she'd been remembering so vividly as to feel she was with him again, forty years ago. Nothing the minister was saying was actually false or wrong, and it was all based, of course, on what she and Ian had told him—such as they could.

So, you might say, this was all their fault.

It was all going to be a performance, just a performance, a pretence. And, despite her resolution not to, she squeezed her mother's hand, because she felt that her mother must be thinking, too, that it was all just a performance and a pretence, and must feel embarrassed and disappointed and dismayed. Even cheated.

How wise her mother had been not to go with them to see the minister, and thus to have as little to do with any of this as possible.

Now the minister was drawing to a conclusion. He hadn't spoken for too long or said too much, which must have been a relief to Ian, but he was finishing on a strong note. Ted Holroyd had been 'a family man, a true family man', he was saying. And he was saying it with a beaming expectation of approval, as if he were presenting a prize.

What did it mean: 'a family man'? What on earth did it mean? Of course he'd been a family man. He'd had a family. He'd fathered—grandfathered—a family. So had millions. And this wasn't something that she and Ian had suggested: 'You could say he was "a family man".' It was the minister's own flourish. It was what you said when you couldn't think of anything else, and how many times had this man said it before?

She saw Betty Sykes again, in her doorway. No one ever spoke of 'a family woman'.

And now she squeezed her mother's hand all the more, because she felt her mother must be doubly embarrassed, worse than embarrassed. Though suppose her mother thought that her hand was being squeezed because of the fine remark the minister had just made?

In any case, her mother's hand didn't squeeze back. It remained like something not even attached to her mother.

'Aye,' Joe Short had said. 'It's one of 'inges. But best to replace whole set. All showing their age. Just like you and me, eh, Ted?'

Clearly, the two men knew each other. Perhaps they'd once been at school together, like her and Sally. Perhaps Joe Short and her father, she thought now, as she sat beside her mother, had got up to tricks together in their younger days. Perhaps she might have said when she'd gone with Ian to see the minister, 'Well, he was quite a one, you know, when he was young, quite the lad, quite a tearaway . . .'

Across the road, the Sykeses, at number 33, must have seen Joe Short's van arrive and seen that something was going on with the Holroyds' front door.

'But not like you, eh, lass?'

Joe Short's eyes had turned on her, as if she were not just a small incidental bystander but part of the conversation. And what a look. He was past his prime, he'd just said so, but still—by her own recognition—a good-looking man. His sleeves were rolled up and his brown forearms, fleeced with dark hair, looked wholly sure of what they were doing.

The first time she'd been attracted to—excited by—a grown-up man.

In the playground, the following Monday morning, Sally Sykes had said, or rather chanted, 'Joe Short, Joe Short! Never went short! That's what my mammy said!'

Sally's feet hadn't missed the rhythm of her skipping-rope.

Joe Short had said that he'd have to go to Ackerley's to get a new set of hinges. But not before, with those arms, he'd unscrewed the door from its current hinges, held it up for a moment, as if he might have danced with it, then placed it on its side, for better inspection, under the front window.

'Nowt wrong with wood. Just 'inges. Ackerley's. Ten minutes. Then I'll have it back up in no time. You could put kettle on meanwhile.'

But her mother hadn't put any kettles on.

'Joe Short, Joe Short! Never got caught! That's what my mammy said!'

And Sally's mother had seemed to know Joe Short quite well.

Off went 'J. Short' in his van, leaving the two of them lingering again in the now empty doorway. It was a sort of shock, a violation, the door so suddenly removed—a mere airy gap where it had been—and then placed on its side, like something spurned, against the front wall. The first time, perhaps, in ninety years that it had been so treated.

Her father had looked not a little put-out. Was it this sudden desecration? Or was it that he was thinking that if it was just the hinges, he might have attempted the job himself? How much was this going to come to? And did Joe know what he was on about, anyway? So bloody sure of himself.

Or was it that he'd noticed that she had—noticed—Joe Short?

For whatever reason—to divert attention?—she'd taken her father's hand again and said, looking at the object in question, 'Poor door.'

'Poor door. Poor *door*!' Her father had suddenly chuckled. 'Oh, aye, Annie, no knocking on it now, is there, no letting us in or out? Poor door, all right.'

Her strange lamenting remark had lifted him from his thoughtfulness. She'd made, it seemed, a sort of joke. But then, as if she were in genuine sorrow for the door, he'd squeezed her hand and said, 'Don't you fret, Annie. Joe'll have it fixed right enough, just you see.'

His hand had seemed to tingle. She'd squeezed it back, to show that she'd been comforted.

Had he noticed? That she'd noticed. Had he even noticed—though thoughts can't be seen—the question she'd put to herself in her nine-year-old head? Since the two men were there before her, it was a matter of direct comparison. 'Suppose,' she'd asked herself, 'I'd had Joe Short for a father?'

And Sally Sykes, in the playground, if she'd been older than her years and not just constantly parroting her mother, might have said, 'Well, you nearly might have done.'

She'd stood with her father in the doorway, a breeze blowing in, sun on their faces, looking at the stricken item. Had he always remembered her 'Poor door', kept it inside him? Was it with him even now, in his coffin?

Ian had got up and gone to the lectern to deliver his 'few words'. He still hadn't told her what he was going to say, yet she had an idea, and felt that he'd make a decent job of it.

He would say that the Holroyds were Yorkshire people, though they'd all moved down, some while ago, to the 'soft south'. And he'd make a sort of joke out of this desertion. That was the thing, on a serious occasion, to make a sort of joke. To ease the tension. But then he'd nonetheless say, turning serious, that Ted Holroyd was a true Holroyd and a true, proud Yorkshireman. Even in the soft south, Ted Holroyd had always remained a staunch supporter of Huddersfield Town . . .

Or something like that.

And this was more or less what Ian did say and, yes, he made a good job of it. The minister's 'family man' had even given him a useful lead-in. And yet—poor Ian—none of his eulogy seemed to ring true either; it was all just another performance, though a good one. And she knew that she must never let slip to Ian any hint that she'd thought this.

But now it was her turn to go to the lectern. Her brother had said, in an oddly chivalrous way, 'And now my sister, Anne, is going to read a poem.'

But did she have to? Really? It said so in the Order of Service. It was expected, so she had to. The poem was even printed in its entirety in the Order of Service, which meant that people would have already read it. So did she have to read it again?

There had been a decision to print the whole poem, since it would fill out the little leaflet and make it more like something people might want to keep. On the front was a photo of Ted Holroyd ('Edward James Holroyd') in his handsome early twenties. More handsome than Joe Short?

In truth, there was nothing special about the poem. It was just a poem that, in the end, because she'd said she'd read a poem, she'd picked from a list: Best Poems to Read at a Funeral.

In that playground, long ago, there'd been a saying: true as tripe. Or was it one of those things that Sally's mammy had said? Where was Betty Sykes now? And where was Sally? Had Sally Sykes grown up to look exactly like her mother? And had she, Annie Stevens, formerly Holroyd, grown up to look exactly like hers?

Was that what people would mainly be thinking as she stood in front of them, reading a poem: Doesn't she look just like her mother?

She got up and walked forward with her folded piece of paper. Did she have to? Didn't she have the right, as the dead man's daughter—his nine-year-old daughter—to change her mind, even at the last moment? And wouldn't doing something on the spur of the moment, because she simply couldn't help it, ring more true?

No, I'm not going to read a poem. You can all read it anyway, on the page in front of you. You probably already have. No, I want to tell you instead about a memory I have of my father, from a long time ago, when I was a small girl. I want to give you—well, a sort of sketch of my father.

She walked towards the lectern. Was this what the minister had meant by 'breaking down'? Not being able to carry on. But she hadn't even begun yet. What was the signal for that?

Or: she might read, after all, a different sort of poem. A very short one, though, in its way, a perfect poem. Nothing but rhyme. Not even read it, just say it. She might just say, looking at all their astonished faces, or perhaps—better—looking at the coffin: 'Poor door.'

She reached the lectern. She took a breath. She unfolded her piece of paper on which were the same words that were printed in the Order of Service. She smiled bravely, like a small girl called to the front of the class. She cleared her throat, then read the poem that everyone was expecting and would approve of, saying later to her that it was a lovely poem to have chosen and that she'd read it very well.

VII

FIREWORKS

Fireworks

It was late October 1962. Russian missiles were being shipped to Cuba. Kennedy was having words with Khrushchev. The world might be coming to an end.

It was a common remark: 'Cheer up, it's not the end of the world.'

Frank Green's wife, Joan, had just said to him, a look of genuine fear on her face, 'Is the world going to end, Frankie?'

He said, 'Don't be silly.'

He'd nearly said, 'How should I know?' But that would have sounded flippant. His wife looked truly distraught.

'Will it come to an end before the wedding?'

Had she really said that?

'Sophie's shut herself in her bedroom. She won't let me in. She's in tears. We were going to collect the dress this week.'

'Well, collect it.'

It was a Tuesday evening. Frank, like many people, dreaded Mondays, but by Tuesday he could usually be quite good-humoured. The worst day of the week was over and he was resigned to all the others.

But this was no ordinary week. His daughter, Sophie, was getting married in less than a fortnight. Everything was ready. He'd forked out huge sums of money, but that wasn't the point. He ought to be sailing serenely through the days ahead. At work, they'd been saying to him, 'Big event getting near, eh, Frank?'

But now, apparently, the end of the world would intervene.

He said again, with perhaps a gentler but more commanding tone, 'Don't be silly.' The look on Joan's face was real. The news on the TV was real.

'I'll go and see if she'll let me in.'

'You do that.'

Frank did something he'd never done before. Standing in front of his wife, he gripped her by the shoulders with his two hands. With hardly any force, but deliberately, he shook her. As if to say, 'Snap out of it.'

He realised that he was dealing with a state of incipient panic. The air was crackling around him. He understood that his wife must do with their daughter something like what he was doing with his wife now. If she could get into Sophie's bedroom.

Their daughter was nineteen and about to get married. She was also the child who'd once thrown an almighty tantrum, on her ninth birthday, because it was chucking it down and the promised birthday picnic was not to occur.

He remembered the tantrum. How could he forget? He remembered his own misery at having no power over the weather.

'Tell her everything's all right. And tell her. . . tell her it's not our fault.'

Why had he said that? It wasn't his daughter's fault, no. So whose fault was it but the older generation's? The one he and Joan belonged to.

No sooner had his wife gone to see if she could gain access to their daughter than the phone rang. He picked up, and it was Tony Hammond, Sophie's father-in-law to be.

Tony got straight to the point.

'Should we call it off, Frank? Given the situation. Debbie's having fits. Should we call it off?'

'Are you serious?'

Frank took a deep breath. He said, as steadily as possible, 'It can't be called off. It's less than two weeks away. Everything's set up.'

It was a bad answer. It implied that it *might* have been called off. His daughter's wedding might have been sensibly called off at some other time—it was only the lateness that was unreasonable. He should have said, 'It's my daughter's wedding. No one's calling it off.' Or just said, as he'd said to Joan, but with a touch of ferocity, 'Don't be so bloody silly, Tony.'

But he was talking to his daughter's future father-in-law.

Tony said, 'But what if no one comes? Given the situation. They might not come. If we're all still here. They might not come if there's still a situation.'

Was he hearing correctly? He formed a picture of all the guests he'd invited to his daughter's wedding not showing up because they were glued to their radios, poised to sprint to the nearest bunker. Wherever such things were supposed to be.

If we're all still here? Well, of course they wouldn't come if they weren't 'here'.

'They'll all be in a dilemma, Frank, and they might not turn up.'

Dilemma? Situation? There was something in Tony's voice not unlike the look that had been on Joan's face. He realised that Tony believed what he was saying. He believed in the 'situation'. Why would he have phoned up otherwise?

So was he, Frank Green, the weird exception? The only obstinate non-believer?

A voice inside Frank, deep in his guts, was now saying, 'This isn't happening, this can't be happening.' It was the same insistent voice that he'd heard inside him when he was a bomb-aimer, lying on his knotted stomach, above various German cities. He'd spent more than twenty years trying to avoid the memories. Now Tony Hammond was bringing them all back.

He couldn't shake Tony by the shoulders, but he wouldn't have wanted to.

A sudden rage surged through Frank against this man who purported to be the father of the man Sophie was marrying. He'd met him quite a few times, met his wife, Deborah, who was, apparently, at this moment, 'having fits'. (Though so, apparently, was Sophie.) Tony Hammond, in all honesty, didn't mean a lot to Frank, but it had been necessary that they become friends.

Now this same man was rapidly becoming an enemy. Yet it was extremely important that he, Sophie's father, shouldn't let loose at him. It was vital, in fact, that he should treat him as an even more significant friend.

Was this how it was with Kennedy and Khrushchev?

Frank had the thought: Now they can do it all with missiles. They don't have to send hundreds of men up into the air to die.

He said, patiently and calmly, 'No one's calling off my daughter's wedding just because the world's going to end.' Had he really said that? 'In any case, Tony, you can take it from me, you can rest assured. The world's not going to end, I promise you. Stay calm. We'll all be here next week.'

Had he really said those words? How the hell did he actually know? Did he even have the right to know—to promise? Was he God?

'And we'll all be *there* on the Saturday. At the church. You know how to get there? Give my best to Deborah. Tell her to stay calm. And my best to Steve, of course.'

Tony hadn't mentioned the condition of Steve, the bridegroom. Was he cowering under a table?

People could get into total flaps about weddings. Frank knew this. It was common knowledge. But he'd never before faced the wedding of his own daughter. He'd spoken as if he'd already arranged this wedding many times, been present at it often, so, this time, he had it sorted. There's doing things and there's having to do them again and again. Such thinking doesn't, or shouldn't, apply to weddings.

The truth was it was all entirely new to him and part of him was terrified. Even without the end of the world, he'd have been terrified.

But he was right. The wedding did happen. The end of the world didn't. By the crucial Saturday, it was clear that Kennedy and Khrushchev had come to an understanding. The world could breathe again. The wedding was only made more special, more jubilant—the pealing of bells, the scattering of confetti—by everyone's recognition that the world hadn't ended.

His daughter hadn't looked like a grizzling girl. She'd looked like Grace Kelly.

Then the wedding was over. Time moved on. The event itself would be indelible, but all that preparation and anxiety were done with. The bride and groom, now Mr and Mrs, were still on their honeymoon (something else that hadn't been cancelled) and Frank and Joan Green were getting used to the fact—it was clearly going to take time, it was a whole new phase of life—that it was now 'only them'.

It was November, darkness pressing in—the time for the wearing of poppies and the time of Guy Fawkes Night.

Frank still had his old sheepskin-leather Irvin flying jacket, and he'd slip it on now and then to do odd jobs around the house when the weather turned chilly: sweep the leaves from the back lawn, wash the car, climb up a ladder to clear out the gutters.

It was not so strange to see men who'd turned forty wearing such things. It was evidence that they could still get into them, that they'd not lost the physique of their youth. Frank hardly thought now of the circumstances in which he'd once worn this jacket. It had become just a familiar domestic item that hung on a hook in the garage.

If someone had said to him all those years ago, 'One day you'll wear this jacket to sweep up the leaves in your garden . . .'

But who could possibly have said that?

If asked why he still wore his wartime flying jacket, he might have blinked a bit and said, 'It's a good jacket.'

Every fifth of November, for a few years now, he had

put on his flying jacket and gone along to the Harpers', at number 20, for their Guy Fawkes Night. Sometimes, but not usually, Joan and Sophie would go with him. Bob and Kate Harper had two small boys, so Guy Fawkes Night in their garden was a fixture. He and Joan, with just their one daughter, had never made an event of it.

It was a chance, Frank was well aware of it, to go back to his own boyhood. How he'd loved Guy Fawkes Night—Bonfire Night, as it was usually called. How he could remember still, across all the accumulating years, the annual thrill of it. The magic of a box of fireworks.

Bob and Kate had been at the wedding, and Frank, in his father-of-the-bride regalia, had said to them, 'I suppose I'll see you on Monday. If you'll still have me. Not dressed like this, of course.'

Kate had laughed and said, 'Why not?'

Frank had seen himself, in his tailed morning suit, standing by a bonfire.

The fifth of November happened to be a Monday—those days Frank detested. But Monday evenings set you straight again. When he came home from work, he double-checked with Joan.

She said, 'Go on. Off you go.'

He felt almost at once that he was doing the wrong

thing. He should have said, 'I think I'll give it a miss this time, Joanie.'

He could tell from Joan's voice that she was thinking: Isn't it high time he gave up this annual foible of his? She was thinking: Sophie's not here, and now he's slouching off for his fireworks.

But Frank also felt that, this year, he wanted to go all the more. It was fifty yards down the road and he'd be gone for an hour. He was hardly leaving Joan all alone like a widow, and why couldn't she come, too?

Sophie had left them. They'd known it would happen one day. It wasn't the end of the world.

Though as Frank, in his flying jacket, walked along to Bob and Kate's, things were already starting to go flash and bang all around him. There was a smell of smoke.

Centuries ago there'd been a Gunpowder Plot. That hadn't transpired, either.

Bob, in outdoor scruffs, opened the door and ushered him straight through to the garden. Kate was there with the two boys—both of them hopping with excitement. She looked like someone restraining two dogs on leads. She'd just lit a firework. She waved and grinned. She wore a woollen pompom hat. The bonfire was already ablaze.

The 'Guy' on top of it, a figure in an old pair of pyjamas and a crayoned cardboard mask, was calmly awaiting incineration.

There was the sudden dazzle and sizzle of the firework.

Bob said, 'Quite a show on Saturday.'

Frank said, 'Glad you were there.'

'We wouldn't have missed it.'

'And I wouldn't miss this.'

For the Harpers, these November visits of Frank's were simply an open invitation, a tradition—including the wearing of the flying jacket. They didn't question why he usually came alone. They may have thought, without any judgement: He just wants to be a boy again.

'How's Joan?' Bob said.

'Fine. Sends her best.'

'I'll get you something to keep the cold out.'

Frank laughed. 'There's a blazing fire, Bob, to keep the cold out.'

But then Bob was besieged by the boys and their mother, begging him to set off a rocket. It was a grown-up man's job to set off rockets. They were launched from an empty milk bottle.

Frank said, 'Off you go.'

He stood and watched. The garden was juddering in

the light from the bonfire. Bob crouched with a match box while Kate held the boys back. There was the usual tense moment when everyone thought nothing was going to happen. Then, as if with a mind of its own, the rocket whizzed up and did its glittery burstings, to oohs and ahs.

Frank had the sudden outrageous feeling that he wouldn't have minded if Bob and Kate had become Sophie's parents-in-law. Outrageous and, of course, impossible. Which one of those two prancing boys would have married his daughter?

But Bob wouldn't have phoned up to rant hysterically.

The worn leather of his flying jacket glinted like metal. When it hung, on its own, in the garage, its sleeves retained their bends. No one could have said to him, either, all those years ago, 'One day, you'll wear that jacket to watch fireworks on Guy Fawkes Night, two days after your daughter's wedding.'

He'd stood outside the church, in his finery, in crisp autumn sunlight, his heart pounding as he ceremonially offered Sophie his arm. She was spectacularly dressed. Days before, she'd shut herself in her bedroom. Now, it was as if she'd stroked his wrist and said, 'Everything will be all right, Dad.'

There was the irrevocable sound of the organ starting

up inside, the scuffling noise of the congregation rising to its feet.

It should have been the last thing he'd ever want to do: wear his old flying jacket and stare into flames, watch fireworks.

And the truth was that if, back then, he could have been, in some impossible way, both there and not there, just a safe, immune spectator, he might have been able to say that, on a grand and terrible scale, that was just what it was like: immense bonfires burning below, and up in the sky a great show—flashes and bangs, coloured flares, dancing searchlight beams.

His inner voice had said, 'You're not really here. This isn't happening.'

His actual voice had said, 'Steady, Skip . . . hold her . . . not yet . . . not yet . . .'

He needed to be getting back to Joan. All the feverish anticipation, then everything was soon over. The 'Guy' was no more. The bonfire was a collapsing orange pyre.

But, before he could make his departure, Bob, with apologies, plonked a steaming mug into his hand. 'Have some of that to see you home.'

See him home? Fifty yards.

He sniffed the steam and recognised the faintly meaty smell. Bob couldn't have known.

'Bovril,' Bob said. 'That is, Bovril with a good slug of Scotch in it. You wouldn't think it would make such a good mix.'

Bovril. Breakfasts. Debriefings and breakfasts. The tea could be awful stewed muck. Not that you were fussy. It was hot and wet and a chance to fill yourself with liquid sugar. But there was usually also Bovril, if you wanted it. It wasn't bad.

Bovril for breakfast. It was the taste of safety, of getting back, of being—for the time being—still alive.

It might have been five in the morning, barely dawn.

In their unbelievable way, those mornings were like Monday evenings. Well, you'd got through that. Now you could adjust to getting through it again.

He took a swig.

Bob said, 'Good?'

'Yes, Bob, very good.'

Even without the slug of Scotch, it would have been very good.

VIII

KIDS

KIDS

Nick and Judy were on holiday, in Cyprus. It was just them. For many years their 'just-themness'—it could seem like a secret formula that only they possessed—had filled them with gratitude and satisfaction. Then it had begun to nag at them, like one of those things you push to the back of your mind.

Was it a sin to feel that life was complete? Was it a mistake to admit to being happy?

Neither Nick nor Judy had been to Cyprus before and neither of them knew much about it. Did it matter? A beach was a beach was a beach. On the long flight out—they hadn't even known that Cyprus was so far away—Nick had told Judy that, when he was little, a neighbour of theirs, Mr Bates, had said to him and his mother one morning that he'd done his national service in Cyprus and that it had been 'nasty' and you could 'get your arse shot off'.

This graphic revelation had left its impression on Nick, though he couldn't have understood it at the time. He couldn't have been more than five.

So he'd said to Judy, just to get them both in the holiday mood, that they were going to a nasty place where they might get their arses shot off. But, of course, what Mr Bates had been referring to had been decades ago, even before he and Judy were born.

When Mr Bates had employed his rough language he'd been clipping his front hedge. You had to stop and say hello to neighbours. Nick could remember that his mother had been holding his hand and as Mr Bates spoke she'd squeezed it tightly, as if to protect him or, in some way, to apologise. Though he didn't tell Judy this. But as he shared with her his appetising memory, he was aware of thinking of himself as a small boy and of presenting to her the image of his five-year-old self, with his mother. And then he'd used the words 'before we were born'.

What had caused Mr Bates to bring up Cyprus at all? Perhaps it was the hot weather. You had to exchange a word or two with neighbours and mentioning the weather was always a good start. Perhaps his mother had said that it was hot, and perhaps Mr Bates had said, 'Hot! When I was in Cyprus . . .'

And then he'd gone off down memory lane.

But he and Judy didn't have to worry about their holiday. They couldn't have found themselves in a less nasty place. Mr Bates might never have wanted to make a return visit, but they couldn't have been in less of a trouble-spot.

And it was hot. It was early October. In London, when they'd left, it had been grey and chilly, but in Cyprus it was still remarkably hot, like a second dose of summer.

And quiet. End of season. The summer crowds had departed. All across Europe, the school summer holidays were over. But since it was just him and Judy, they could take holidays whenever they liked—in late March or early October. Or both. At such times, rates were cheap, but it wasn't a question of cost. They could have afforded to take holidays in high summer. But why take a holiday then, if you didn't want crowds and screaming kids?

And if you didn't want screaming kids, so the argument, until recently, might have gone, why have any of your own?

Just them? It had been an issue. 'Issue' was the right

word. But not any more. They had decided. It was no longer 'if', or even 'when?' This holiday would be unique. It would even be, in a sense, the last one. The last one when it would be just them.

It was October 1999. Nick was thirty-five, Judy thirty-four. If they'd struggled to make their minds up, then more than one ticking clock had persuaded them. They would have kids for the new millennium. What a nice idea. They were still just themselves, and might even be, for one last time, just kids themselves. Wasn't that what holidays were for? For feeling that you were just a kid again.

After they'd taken off from Heathrow and the drinks trolley came round, Nick hadn't been slow in asking for champagne. He'd said to Judy, 'Here's to it!' The 'it' was quite a big it. It embraced more than just their holiday. It embraced a whole millennial plan.

Cold, miserable London was gone. When they stepped, a few hours later, from an airport terminal to their waiting 'transfer' car, they were pleased to feel that, though it was dark, the air was balmy. It seemed to caress. Their driver had said, 'Welcome to Cyprus.' And Nick had said happily to Judy, echoing what his mother had once, perhaps, said to Mr Bates, 'It's hot.'

*

At some point in their lives, the world had started, seriously, to go on holiday. The world had become a pleasure-ground, an offering of sunny destinations—arrival halls opening onto palm trees. It had never been like it in human history before.

And at some point in their lives, something else had happened to the world. It had, of course, got older, yet it had got younger. It had suddenly got young. Thirty-five had once been the traditional mid-point of life. Not any more. My God, to be over the hill at thirty-five! At thirty-five you could still be waiting to be grown-up and a parent. You could still feel eighteen. Or five.

Up on the headland next to this end of the beach was their hotel, with its own secluded pool, if you preferred it. But this end of the beach was anyway hotel-exclusive. Every morning staff tidied it up and rearranged the loungers and umbrellas and the little low tables with legs designed to lodge in the sand.

At the back of the beach and just the right distance from what had now become 'their' spot was a large cabin affair with decking and awnings and its own kitchen, all run by the hotel. You could get a good lunch. It was called, in English, 'The Paradise Bar'. They were in a Greek-speaking part of the world—wasn't 'paradise' a Greek word?—but everyone spoke English. Every so often, smiling boys or girls in hotel T-shirts, with trays under their arms, would make their way from the Paradise Bar to ask if there was anything they could bring you.

Judy was wearing a black bikini. She was glistening and dripping from their latest dip. 'Dip' was a debatable word. Judy looked fabulous in a black bikini, especially when she'd tanned, which she had by now. They were more or less halfway through their holiday. She tanned more easily and quickly than he did, but he was getting there.

He was wearing a pair of jazzy, holiday-patterned swimming shorts. This year's fashion was quite long. His shorts, he thought, were both ridiculous and appropriate. They made him feel, and perhaps look, not just young, but—boyish. If not five years old. They provided Judy with amusement; she provided him with classic beach-beauty.

It was almost eleven in the morning. They'd been in for a swim. 'Swim' or 'dip'? Another issue. They'd waded back together, returned to their spot, patted and rubbed themselves with towels, and in a moment they might have both settled down on their loungers.

But in their sorties into the sea there was a difference between them. Yes, they would swim and bob around together in all the usual ways, but it was Judy who was the real swimmer. She loved to swim, and was very good at it. He would talk about a 'dip', Judy a 'swim'. After a while he would be ready to do some more basking, while Judy was still up for more swimming.

Fair enough. He would get out. She would stay in and carry on swimming. Once he'd got out, she would really get going, in fact, with her swimming. And, from the beach, he'd watch. He loved to watch Judy swimming. He had no competitive urge to put on any manly aquatic displays of his own. Judy was better at it, a natural, and he loved to watch.

Now and then she might pause and tread water, and they might wave at each other. She might be near enough for him to see the gleam of her smile. But, most of the time, she would be in happy, intent motion. This way and that she would go, now on her front, now on her back, now creating a splash, now not.

She was his wife, but these occasions could make him feel a strange separation, as if she had become unobtainable yet he yearned from afar. A lump could come into his throat. It had always been worth going on these frivolous things called holidays, just to have these moments of almost painful enthralment.

Up and down the beach, there were other women, younger ones, girls, in bikinis. They caught the eye. But he loved to watch his wife. It was a truth: he only had eyes for her.

He should say this. He should say it to her. But there were things you could say that, when you said them, might only sound silly. There were things you could say, but should keep inside, unless and until they found their moment. Then you could say them.

It looked as if he'd be doing some watching now.

After this first 'dip' of the morning—it hadn't really been a swim—they'd simply waded out together. It could sometimes happen like that. Judy's concession to him. But then, after getting back to their loungers and even after some towelling down, Judy might say, as she said now, 'I think I'll go back in.'

Fair enough. It was an odd little quirk, but it could happen too. He wondered why Judy did it, but no problem. They were on holiday and should both do as they pleased.

'Fair enough,' he said. 'Don't let me stop you.' He smiled. He didn't say, 'Why didn't you just stay in?' Which would have been slightly argumentative and unnecessary. 'I'll watch,' he said. He was really quite happy with his wife's change of plan.

'No you won't,' Judy said, smiling as well. 'You'll lie back and fall asleep.'

True, he might. Though who was being argumentative now? But a little mild and teasing argumentativeness, on holiday, could be quite nice.

'Maybe I will, maybe I won't.' He shrugged, reaching for his sunglasses. 'Off you go,' he said in a slightly permissive, fatherly way.

'Well, be careful,' Judy said. 'Put some stuff on. Don't burn.' Tanned herself, she could fuss, unnecessarily, about his own more reluctant skin. She spoke in a slightly motherly way.

Nick thought: Look at us. We've made our decision, now we're practising being parents on each other.

He perched his sunglasses on his nose. 'I won't burn,' he said. 'I won't even smoke.' An in-joke.

Then he settled back, his lounger not yet fully lowered. And he did indeed watch his wife as she retraced her steps over the sand, entered the water and, after just a few eager strides, plunged forward to be wholly—in her element.

She was a marine creature. He was clearly a land animal.

Then he lowered the back of his lounger and reclined fully. He loved to watch, but he loved also that delicious sensation, after a 'dip', of letting the sun dry you and cocoon you in a soporific warmth that was not yet pressing heat. He removed the sunglasses he'd just put on, better to feel the sun on his closed eyelids. All he could see now was a glowing orange.

Nick had an older brother, Mark. Mark was a partner in a travel company—Holden's Holidays—and was raking it in. It was Mark who fixed up the highly discounted yet high-end holidays for Nick and Judy. It was an arrangement that was hard to refuse.

It was Mark who'd said recently that they might do worse than Cyprus. Far enough south to be still warm in October. And had backed up his suggestion with the two-page spread in his brochure—the top-of-the-range one, the 'Boutique Collection'. Nick and Judy only had to look at the glossy pictures and say yes. Mark's recommendations had never failed before. There was no need to ask if it would come at the usual rate.

What a good daddy of a big brother Mark could be, and what spoilt but grateful children—sent off to play again—Nick and Judy could be. The irony of it all was that Mark and his wife Barbara didn't, these days, get to do much travelling themselves. Saddled with kids. Two boys and a girl. How had it happened?

Nick worked in advertising. Judy ran a florist's called Blooms. Were Mark and Barbara a good advert for the wisdom of having a family? Their, fortunately, large house was sometimes known to Nick and Judy as 'Pandemonium Hall'. Wise or not, Mark and Barbara didn't seem unhappy, they didn't look as if they'd made a dreadful mistake.

Nick sometimes felt that if he were to ask Mark, 'Don't you miss all the jetting about?' Mark would say, 'Yes, but look what I've got.' So he didn't ask.

Perhaps wisdom didn't come into it. Did wisdom come into anything much? Advertising was not a trade of the wise.

Not long ago, Nick had worked on a campaign for Carson's, the 'baby-products' people. Specifically, the 'nappies' people. Carson's had wanted a complete remake that, among other things, got clean away from that—unattractive—word.

Nick, all by himself (and, in fact, in a matter of seconds), had come up with the innocuous word 'cosies'. Cosies! 'Carson's Cosies'. It even had a ring. For this brainwave, Carson's had paid undisclosed sums, and Nick had received a small bonus and pats on the back. But he'd been careful to insist that his flash of inspiration had really been the result of 'team-work'.

Cosies! Had it been a sign? An omen?

Everywhere, there would be ads employing the comfortable new word. No one—including his indulgent older brother—need know that it was his, Nick Holden's, word. The irony was that, whatever name the wretched things went by, it had been Mark and Barbara who, until quite recently, had been up to—well, their arses in them. It had been too late to organise for them, in at least part repayment for the holidays, regular free supplies of Carson's Cosies.

When Nick had first met Judy he'd thought: Who wouldn't want to work in flowers? It was the perfect job. But he'd already signed up for a career in advertising. If everyone worked in flowers, the world would surely be a better place. It was like the thought you could have on holiday: Why couldn't life *always* be like this?

But there were those who worked in advertising who claimed that advertising was constantly striving to make the world a better place.

Around the time that the holiday in Cyprus had been planned, Nick had made a bet with his older brother. Just a verbal bet, not a real one. 'I bet you the year 2000 will turn out to be much the same as the year 1999.' Didn't life generally turn out to be much the same as it had been before? Mark had said, 'You're probably right. But one thing's for certain, we won't be getting any younger.'

'Speak for yourself,' Nick might have said. But he knew when and when not to talk back to Mark. The incontestable fact was that he would always be younger than his big brother. He and Judy would always be younger than Mark and Barbara. It was in their nature to be not just young—but younger! And, for the time being, to be just them.

He hadn't said to Mark, though he might have done, that one significant thing would be different. He and Judy would become parents. So, in a way, his bet had been a lie. Though can you lie about something that hasn't yet happened? He'd hedged his bet.

He hadn't said, 'I bet you, Mark, that Judy and I will have kids.' He hadn't thought it was the moment, and he hadn't wanted his dependable older brother to get all patronising and smug.

The 1990s. Their good-time years, their holiday years. Mainly thanks to Mark.

*

He opened his eyes. Blinked. Looked out to sea. There was Judy, instantly discernible, dashing and splashing this way and that. On their holidays these might be the only times when they were actually apart. Otherwise, they were pretty much joined at the hip.

As if sensing his renewed gaze, Judy stopped in her swimming, turned towards the beach and raised an arm to wave. Her face flashed and glittered.

A blue sea, a blue sky. What more could you want than all this? Was paradise such a long shot?

He raised a hand and waved back. Beyond his sea-happy wife, in the distance, was that thing, a meeting of blues, that you usually only saw on holidays, and then didn't think about much. The horizon. Another Greek word? He waved. He might have been waving goodbye to their 'just-them' years. He might have been waving to some idolised daughter, the image of her mother. 'Look at me—I can swim!'

Once—not so long ago either—Nick had been a smoker. He'd been a smoker, in fact, though no one need know, since he was fourteen or fifteen. When he and Judy had got married he was already a seasoned user of tobacco. But, clearly, she wasn't going to make it a condition. Will I marry you? Only if you stop smoking. It was what he came with. He must have come with some other things that she liked. She didn't smoke herself. Yet she signed up to be a passive smoker, and never demanded or moaned.

Nonetheless, it niggled. Was it fair of him? Did he really have a leg to stand on? His position was, unsurprisingly, that he'd give up smoking—one day. Not yet. It seemed to him, sometimes, that it was a bit like the issue of having kids. Though that was about starting, not stopping.

Because Judy had her florist's business, their house—their smallish house, but big enough for just a couple—was readily full of flowers. It was a little like the holidays. Everything came as if on special offer.

So there was always, without Judy having to say anything, the strong, even reproachful, in-your-face argument: You live in a house full of flowers and you want to *smoke*? To flick ash and stub out the nasty little remnants, in a house full of flowers? You have a house full of flowers, a beautiful wife and you go on high-end holidays, and you want to *smoke* as well?

Mr Bates, Nick suddenly remembered as he leant back on his lounger, had smoked. Even as he clipped his front hedge, that sunny morning, he'd smoked. Even as he talked about Cyprus there was a cigarette dangling from the corner of his mouth.

Yes, but not yet. Time had gone by. Nick worked in an office in a congenial Regency building, just north of Oxford Street, where—although, generally, offices were starting to get strict—everyone smoked all the time to their heart's content.

Yes, but not yet. Then the approaching millennium had begun to seem like his unavoidable, though quite lenient deadline. It still gave him three or four years. Yes, he'd stop smoking—for the new millennium. Make a big thing of it. Throw a party. Not a new-year resolution, but a new-millennium one. How about that?

Though he hadn't got round to announcing any of this to Judy quite yet.

Then his agency had moved office. From the smoke-friendly haven, not so far from Soho, to the ninth floor of a glass tower in Docklands. It was 1997. Business was expanding and it was deemed the thing to do. One small snag. You couldn't smoke. A flat, no-ifs-and-buts prohibition. Or you *could* smoke, if you were prepared to go down nine floors, endure whatever weather was outside and do all this, somehow, not on company time.

Nick had decided that the moment had come. If you

can't beat them, join them. The non-smokers, that is. And no fanfares. He'd simply said to Judy one day, 'I'm giving up. I'm stopping smoking.'

She might have fallen off her chair. A look—an extraordinary succession of looks—came over her face. Gladness, relief and something else, as if some new, until now closed dimension had opened up in her life.

He understood, all at once, that it was worth giving up smoking (though he hadn't *done* it yet) just to see this transfiguration. To see Judy becoming *more* Judy. With such an incentive to help him, he did indeed give up. And found it not to be the torment he'd supposed. What had all his shilly-shallying been about?

And he'd done it without any millennium to hold him to it. In that respect it was different from the kids thing. With the kids thing it had become an undeniable, if unspoken understanding. It stared them *both* in the face. Yes, for the new millennium. If not then, when? A glaring, all-lights-flashing target, in fact. How many holidays did you need? How much happiness did you have to save up before you could say: Now the world will belong to our kids?

But it still needed saying. And he somehow understood, though he didn't know why, that it was for him to say it. If you mean something, say it. So he'd said it. He'd said one day, 'Let's have kids, Jude. Let's go on holiday this autumn and have kids for the new millennium. How about that?'

The same look, the same wave of looks, had come over her face. But redoubled. So: had his giving up smoking only been a sign? Like Carson's Cosies?

And, again, was it such a big deal? Such a drive over a cliff? Though, of course, this had only been the declaration, the intention. It hadn't *happened* yet.

This, right now, was all still their honeymoon time, as it were. Or, as they might come to think of it, their 'Cyprus time'.

As he lay on his lounger, only now and then would his fingers itch and twitch for the pack of cigarettes that wasn't there. It could seem like something that only his hand felt deprived of.

He stretched out again. He'd looked and he'd watched. There she'd been, even waving back at him. How wonderful. After all, he might have looked and Judy might *not* have been there. Then what? Then this holiday, this piece of paradise, would have turned into hell. But she'd been there. And she'd be there still, in the water, he estimated, for another ten to fifteen minutes yet.

He didn't know much about Cyprus, but he knew one thing. It had loomed from his dormant general knowledge not long after this holiday was booked. It was the birthplace of Venus. It was where Venus had been born—or, rather, *not* born, since, apparently, she'd simply risen, mysteriously and marvellously, in all her adult fully formed glory, from the waves. The goddess of love.

Well, what a happy coincidence and encouragement. What an endorsement.

Every afternoon, after a not too heavy but tipsy lunch in the Paradise Bar, they'd walk up to their hotel for a—siesta. Ho, ho.

It must have been said by countless men holidaying in Cyprus with their wives or girlfriends, and, obvious as it might be, he wasn't going to be left out. Why hadn't he said it already? He hadn't quite been given the right moment yet, perhaps. But he'd been given it now, thanks to Judy's little change of heart. If you mean something, say it. And he must say it now when she reappeared, dripping wet, before him, and he must say it with unalloyed worship: 'Venus risen from the waves.'

He stretched out and continued to bask. Yes, in a moment he'd move the umbrella round and slap on some stuff, but not yet. He'd not had enough delicious drying. He closed his eyes. The world went orange again.

Had Mr Bates, in his days in Cyprus, been aware that he was on the island of love? Apparently not. He, Nick Holden, aged thirty-five, lazing on a sun-baked beach, had never had to do any national service and get sent to trouble-spots, and had never in his whole life been close to hostility, warfare or violence of any kind.

But, no, that wasn't quite true. Only quite recently, IRA bombs might have gone off in London at any time. In fact, one such bomb, a big one—killing and injuring—had gone off in Docklands, not long before his agency had relocated. Too late to back out. The contracts had been signed. They'd all be moving into a war zone, just because it was considered the smart place to be. You'd think they might have said: Well, if you're nervous about it, we'll let you still smoke.

Had Mr Bates smoked a lot in Cyprus? It was a pretty safe bet. He'd smoked while he talked, still wielding, rather menacingly, his shears. His mother had so earnestly, protectively squeezed his hand, as if she might have said, 'Don't listen, Nicky.' He must have been no more than five. It was before he went, following Mark, to primary school. All Saints Primary School. During the day it was just his mother and him.

His mother, he realised now, would have stepped in front of him to save him from the blast of a bomb.

His mother ... Mr Bates ... the goddess of love ...

He knew that his mind was starting to drift in strange unpredictable directions, in the way it would before he fell asleep.

His mother ... All Saints Primary School ... Miss Beckett ...

Miss Beckett! Where had she sprung from? But there she was, their teacher, only a 'Miss' but old enough to be a grannie, standing before the blackboard and telling them all, with her motherly smile, how, once upon a time, King Alfred—silly old fool—had burnt some cakes ...

Was he awake? Was he asleep? Had he been dreaming of Miss Beckett or just thinking about her? Had she just risen, like Venus, from the waves? He opened his eyes. He stared at the blue water.

Judy *wasn't there*. She'd gone. She wasn't there. He looked again. She *wasn't there*. There were other bobbing heads and splashing bodies, but he'd have known at once which one was Judy's.

A bolt, a burning bolt went through him. He sat bolt upright. At the same time—but it wasn't the same thing—something icy struck, stung his hot shoulders. It was water. Only water, it was how you put out a fire. Splashes of water! His body writhed, as if he'd been scalded. He heard a laugh, a familiar laugh.

He understood. Understood everything. The bolt withdrew, exquisitely, yet it might leave a scar for ever.

He heard Judy's voice.

'My God, I never thought I'd make you jump so much!' Her voice seemed to change from pleasure to pain in the space of a few words.

'Jesus Christ, Jude! Jesus Christ!'

He understood. Everything was all right. He understood. Judy had played that quite common beach trick, a trick that kids played on each other or, more riskily, on some comatose adult.

Adults, it seemed, could play it on each other too.

'Jesus Christ, Jude!'

She must have stepped, stealthily, up the sand, then round behind him while he'd been lying there with his eyes shut, then shaken her wet hands and arms over him.

But which of the two things that had happened—or not happened—had happened first? It seemed that they'd happened both at once.

'Jesus Christ, Jude! Jesus Christ!'

He could get no other words out.

'Okay, okay! Don't be angry!' Judy said. 'It was only my little—game.'

Then, for some reason, she said, quite vehemently, '*We're on holiday!*'

'I'm not angry, I'm not angry—I'm—'

'You looked fast asleep.'

'I wasn't fast asleep.'

'You looked like you'd fallen asleep and I thought you were going to burn. I told you—'

'You thought *I* was going to *burn*?'

The way he said this must have been inexplicable to her.

'So I got out and came up the beach. For your bloody sake! Then when I saw you lying there—well, I couldn't resist.'

'You couldn't resist!'

He realised that all this—the wanderings of his mind: Mr Bates, his mother, Miss Beckett, the memories of thirty years ago—must have occurred in perhaps three minutes. Instead of staying in for maybe fifteen, Judy had seen him apparently falling asleep, so she'd taken steps. Literally. To save him, apparently, from burning.

'Jesus Christ, Jude!'

She'd never know. And now she must think that he was throwing a colossal fit just because of some splashes of water.

He felt his heartbeats beginning to slow.

'It was only a joke. *We're on holiday!*'

That absurd statement again.

'I know. I know we're on holiday. I haven't burnt. Look.'

And wouldn't have burnt. Did it matter that he wouldn't have burnt? She'd *thought* he was going to burn. She'd had his burning in mind.

'No, not *yet*,' Judy said. 'Thanks to me.'

She was now standing before him. She picked up the towel from her lounger. She was dripping wet. And beautiful and precious. And angry.

He was angry too. He didn't understand how his anger had arisen when, in his case, what he was feeling wasn't anger at all, but something at the opposite end of the scale from anger. She was there before him. They were on holiday!

It took a while for everything to subside, to calm down. It took some repositioning of the sun umbrellas. It took, in his case, some demonstrative application of sun cream. But hadn't he tanned quite well already, if not as well as her? Wasn't her concern just a bit overdone?

Hadn't they both been behaving, in fact, a bit like idiotic children?

It took some batting away, on her part, when he'd tried to wrap her with fond urgency in her towel. But he so much wanted to do it, as if he'd rescued her.

It took a visit from a smiling girl from the Paradise Bar, asking what drinks they'd like. Her smile seemed a little unsure. Had she come at the right time?

It took some drinks.

But the sun shone. The waves lapped. Finally, they were both, rather exhaustedly and even dreamily, reclining. Were they *both* now, to cap it all, going to go to sleep?

They were on holiday.

Judy said, but gently this time, 'But you looked fast asleep.'

He said, trying to say it softly, yieldingly, too, 'I wasn't fast asleep. Just—far away.'

'Far away? Where?'

This was tricky. Was it wise for him now to play a bit of a game himself? But if they were on holiday, did wisdom come into it?

'As a matter of fact,' he said, 'I was thinking of Miss Beckett.'

There was a pause.

'Miss Beckett?' Judy said. 'I don't like the sound of that.' Then she said, 'No wonder I made you jump.'

They were lying on their separate loungers, each on their backs, their eyes closed, not looking at each other at all, yet talking, as couples, strangely, even in a double bed can sometimes talk.

He said, 'You don't have to worry, Jude. She was my teacher at primary school. She must have been getting on for fifty even then.'

As he said it he wondered what Miss Beckett might have looked like when she was, say, eighteen. He wondered if she was now alive or dead.

He said again, 'You don't have to worry, Jude.'

But he had the sudden thought that, one day, he and Judy would be fifty. Fifty—and with kids. How many? And, by then, those kids would be in their teens. And how might it have been turning out, the new millennium—*their* millennium?

And would fifty, by then, seem only like thirty-five?

One thing was for certain, no one got any younger. But another thing was for certain, you couldn't ask your kids if they were ready to be born. You could only try hard, before they were born, to imagine what it might be like, one day, to be them.

'All Saints School,' his mother had said. 'Well, I must have two little saints.'

Quite soon, this holiday, which wasn't quite the same as all the others, would be over. He didn't really want to think about it. Soon, even a whole millennium would be over.

'All good things come to an end.' His mother had said that too, quite often. Moments for saying it seemed to keep cropping up. But don't all mothers say it? One day Judy would say it. Life isn't, after all, just one long holiday.

But a beach is a beach is a beach.

In a little while—he could foresee it, if he couldn't foresee the events of a new millennium—they would go up to the Paradise Bar for their lunch. At their little table on the decking under the awning they would look at each other, and would now and then look—it was natural—across the beach, to the blue water, the bobbing heads of bathers and, beyond them, steady and untroubled, the horizon.

Later that day, he remembered—it suddenly came back to him after all the commotion—that he still hadn't said to Judy that she was like Venus risen from the waves. The particular circumstances, that morning, hadn't, as it proved, allowed it. The moment hadn't arisen.

But there were still several days of their holiday left. And, one day in the future, he imagined, he might say to his children, if the right moment arose, that when he and Judy had decided that they wanted to have them, they'd gone for a holiday, specially, on the island where the goddess of love had been born.

IX

BLACK

BLACK

Once, long ago, she'd done something extraordinary and daring—shocking even. But also fine. Yes, fine. In her heart of hearts where she kept it now, a buried secret, she knew that it was the finest thing that she'd done in her life. She knew that in her life she *had* done something fine.

But what had she actually *done*? Nothing remarkable at all. She had got on a bus. She had sat on a seat, chosen a seat. She was free to do so. You didn't even need to be eighteen to choose a seat. You just needed your fare. And yet she knew it would be enough to send the ripples round Scarwood. Ripples? Waves. She knew that the talk would reach her father inside half an hour. And her father would kill her. Her father would kill her, while her mother would watch and do nothing. Well, let's see.

Who was she daring? Herself or her father? Both. Let's see.

The strange thing was that she had 'seen' everything before it happened. She had never known such power of anticipation. She had 'foreseen'. Her foresight was, in fact, all astonishingly correct. Except in one—astonishing and painful—respect.

You don't know what you can do till you do it? Maybe. You don't know what you have in you? Though, for God's sake, she hadn't known till she sat down next to him that he was such a handsome thing. Thing?

It was August 1944 and she was eighteen. A woman, not a girl. Free to lead her own life. Free to work at Dobson's with Lily and all the other girls—women. It was slave labour, it was 'war effort'. Free as all the boys—men—who were free to be getting called up.

Just watch me, Lily.

Now she was fifty-eight. And how had that happened? It was 1984, not 1944, and she and Greg were watching, on the TV news, something shocking, because it was like a battle. It was primitive, brutal. And when the news had paused for an ad break, Greg had said, 'Well, aren't you glad—relieved at least—that he's not around any more, to see all *that* stuff?'

She knew that Greg had meant her father. But her mind had actually been elsewhere. Men were being chased and brought to the ground and beaten. There were police with helmets, shields, truncheons. Police on charging horses. With dogs. But her mind had been floating away.

Greg was a good man, a decent man who'd never hurt a fly. And their own daughter, Christine, who was grown up now and a mother herself, could never have said, 'My dad will kill me.' It was a decent thought of Greg's, and of course he'd meant her father. Greg was still wondering and keeping watch for some delayed-action grief. Her father had died not long ago, and this month, this June, he would have been seventy-nine. Not bad, for a miner.

'He'll kill me if . . .' Nora had said it enough times to Lily, even when they were quite small girls at school. She didn't really mean it, and she'd often say it with a giggle, a laugh. But it became a habit. Her father wasn't really going to kill her. So why did she keep on saying it?

Nora knew that her father hit her mother. Often. She'd seen it, heard it. And her mother just took it. Bit her lip, buttoned her lips and took it, and sometimes looked at her daughter with a grim, silent look that said: Stay out of this, don't try anything, don't get involved.

Her father had never hit her, his daughter Nora. Not yet. Perhaps he thought daughters were different. He seemed to think, at least, that his daughter was somehow precious, pure and untouchable (which she wasn't), so perhaps he shouldn't touch her himself. Who knew? Perhaps now she was eighteen he might hit her. Eighteen and a woman and free. Free to be hit. Who knew?

But he hit her mother, and had done for years. And her mother took it, which, Nora thought, was her big mistake. Because then he would only do it again, and again. He would think he had the right. It was too late, now, to change the arrangement. And her mother's situation, Nora knew, and Lily knew it too, was not so uncommon.

When the war came, the miners of Scarwood, of course, all stayed at home. They were needed, coal was needed. The miners were never going to be sent off anywhere. And quite a few of the women of Scarwood thought: More's the pity.

If you hit someone, there was always the chance, just the chance, that you might kill them. And now there was a war on, and 'kill' was not such a fanciful word.

Nora knew that her father hit her mother, and Lily knew it and had known it for a long time, because Nora had told her. Careless talk cost lives, apparently. But Lily was Nora's best friend, almost like a sister.

Smoking—since playground days when Lily had first, quite casually one morning, offered Nora a cigarette—had always been on the list of things that Nora's father, Alf Armstrong, would kill her for. That was why, still, though she was eighteen and not a schoolgirl any more, she only smoked, furtively, in Dobson's yard with Lily, and only from the packet Lily kept charge of. It was force of habit. Did her father have spies everywhere? Hardly. And, if he did, why should Dobson's be left out?

While he was down the pit, her father certainly couldn't do any checking up on his daughter. It was one of the blessings of the pit. While they were down there, they were powerless. There was safety. So some of the women thought: Let them stay down there.

Lily didn't have to worry about *her* dad's killing her, because he wasn't a miner and he *had* been sent somewhere. To Africa, of all places. Africa! Where was Africa? But now, in 1944—so Lily and her mother believed—he was somewhere in France. Well, it was closer. Lily's father, Bert Alsop, was—or had been—a tobacconist. He'd merely sold cigarettes to miners. (By 1984 it was known that this was only adding to the ruin of their lungs.) Lily's mother, Rosie Alsop, had become the tobacconist. Lily sneaked from her mother's stock the cigarettes that Nora and Lily smoked at Dobson's. And no doubt Lily's mum turned a blind eye.

Though surely she wasn't blind to other things, and must sometimes have thought: That Maggie Armstrong is just buttoning her lips. Her lips that were sometimes swollen.

Lily and her mum, Nora knew, were always wondering, every day and every night, if their father and husband, Bert, was 'all right'. And Nora quite often, strangely, envied them their constant agony. It was something she simply couldn't have imagined feeling about her own father. And she remembered Bert Alsop—it was a case, by now, of remembering—as a sweet man, a sort of uncle, who you couldn't imagine killing anyone. Though perhaps, for most of five years now, that's exactly what he had been doing. And who knew how unsweetened he might have become? They would never know.

It was a fine, even golden late afternoon at the beginning of August. She and Lily had lingered in Dobson's yard to share a cigarette. If they didn't linger for a ciggy, they'd only have to stand waiting longer at the bus stop. They were both wearing ration-book summer frocks, made of cheap cotton, and they were glad, as always, to be released from the full-length brown aprons they had to wear while they worked at the machines, stitching together large panels of fine white silk. It was a sort of cruel joke. All the stern brown aprons, all the girls—women—and all the fine white silk. Woe betide them if they filched any. But where did it come from in the first place, all the silk? You couldn't ask. It would be careless. And yet there seemed to be increasing quantities of it. Production was being 'stepped up'.

They'd dallied in the yard to share a cigarette. A strange ritual. Like naughty girls at school. Then Lily trod on the end of the cigarette—they were her cigarettes and she always killed them—and they walked together to the bus station, timing it just right. They would be at the end of a queue, but the bus, coming out of the depot and starting its journey, would be empty. There would be seats for all.

As they turned into the bus station and walked across the concourse, they could see that there were already nine or ten people in the queue at their stop. But at this point they might have checked their pace a little, even looked for an instant at each other, mouths possibly agape. This was a moment Nora would never clearly remember, but it was before she began to 'foresee' things, and foresee them quite exactly.

The queue was not really like the normal queue. It was like a random line of people separated, by a good two yards, from the man who was technically first in the line and standing right by the stop. He might have just missed the previous bus and so had to be where he was. This man was in uniform. Not a rare thing at all these days. It was the pale-straw summer uniform of the American air force. Not so common, though not so rare either, and it was the unadorned uniform of a man of lowest rank. What was unusual, at least in Mansfield, Nottinghamshire, even in the summer of 1944, was that this man was black. Nora and Lily had never seen such a thing before. Thing?

It was clear that this man was going to get on their bus— why else was he there?—the bus that would take her and Lily to Scarwood, then go on, eventually, to Bessington, where, as everyone knew by now, there was an airbase. Nora and Lily's first thought might well have been that they were glad that they'd be at the end of the queue and so furthest from the black man. He would be nothing to do with them.

As they continued walking towards their stop (and the black man now must have noticed *them*), they did something they'd done all the time when they were schoolgirls to show and confirm that they were friends, but now, being women, they tried to do less—because it looked girlish. They linked arms. The skirts of their summer frocks swished against each other. Lily's was plain pale blue. Nora's was dark blue with white dots. Her father surely couldn't kill her for wearing dark blue and white dots.

Most women even in cheap summer frocks, on a fine sunny afternoon, can look—well, not bad. Or so they hope. And most men in even a humble plain uniform can look not bad, too. Both Nora and Lily might have had the thought, conflicting with other thoughts or feelings they were having, that the man by the stop didn't look bad. Bad?

They joined the end of the queue. Hardly had they done so than they'd seen, beyond the black man, their bus emerge from the shadows of the depot. Like a plane from a hangar, Nora oddly thought. And then her thoughts had taken their remarkable and daring turn. She'd started to foresee things.

Though, first, she'd had the unexpected thought that the black man, standing by himself at the stop, with everyone backing away from him, must be feeling uncomfortable, and, anyway, being in a strange place far from home, feeling rather bewildered and lost (though he seemed to know which bus to get). So she'd felt unexpectedly sorry for him. Then she'd started to see how things might, could—would—happen.

And so they did, so they all did. Never before in her life had she so predicted and seemed to take hold of events, and perhaps in any life such moments come very rarely, if at all. And even the part of it that she *didn't* predict, the part that took hold of *her*, would be astounding and wonderful—and leave her in misery. Yet, in the end, it would never be forgotten or regretted. And perhaps she'd even foreseen this bit too, or wished it. Silly schoolgirl that she still was.

The bus would pull up. The queue would get on. The black man would get on first, he had to, since he was head of the queue. The bus conductor would perhaps look a little startled, but the black man was a serviceman and would have some kind of pass. And he would sit wherever he liked. He had to, he had first pick. He would take an empty seat and he would sit by the window, leaving a space beside him. Natural behaviour. Everyone else would get on, and they would all do their utmost to sit as far as possible from him. He might try not to notice this. By the time she and Lily got on, there would be a very obvious group of empty seats islanding the black man.

She and Lily would take their own seat, sitting next to each other as usual, and, also, as far as possible from the black man. They would nonetheless stare at him all the time, while pretending not to. With luck, they would sit somewhere behind him, so they wouldn't even have to hide their stares.

But, no, it wasn't going to happen like this.

She and Lily got on. It was all as she'd pictured. The black man was sitting on the right-hand side, roughly halfway along. Beside him, in front of him and behind him were empty seats. He was staring fixedly out of the window. Well, wouldn't you, if you were him?

Lily had got on just ahead of Nora and—keeping, indeed, as far as possible from the black man and behind him—had sat herself down on the left-hand side, by the window, expecting that Nora would, of course, sit beside her.

But, no, she wouldn't. Nora remained standing, swaying, clinging to the seat pole—the bus was now moving off—and she looked at Lily. As Lily looked back, Nora gave a quick but unmistakably meaningful cock of her head towards the black man, and Lily's rapid reaction to this was to raise a widened hand to her widened mouth, her eyes bulging in disbelief. She might have said, if she hadn't clapped her hand to her face, 'You're not going to!'

Nora simply nodded in confirmation. Then Lily lowered her hand and did say something. That is, her lips moved. The bus was now throbbing and chugging and Lily might anyway have wished not to be heard. She said, in an amazed and effortful mime-language, 'You won't dare!' Or so Nora thought. And, now in a committed state of amazement at herself, but also of sure foresight, Nora nodded again. She might have said, but didn't, 'Won't I? Just watch me.'

She turned and walked forward, her bare summer arm now raised so that her hand could slide along the rail above. It was a warm evening. All the bus's windows were part-opened and the bus, heading out of town, was now starting to bowl along. A breeze was blowing, in a rather delicious way, along its interior, fluttering Nora's frock. She had the strange feeling, as she lurched forward, that the bus was taking her to some part of the world where she had never been. And yet she knew, entirely, what she was doing.

Her father would kill her? If he would kill her for smoking or for, say, wearing bright red lipstick, then he would kill her, surely, for this. But he didn't. He wouldn't. She somehow knew, even as she propelled herself along the bus, that if she did something so flagrantly kill-worthy as this, he wouldn't actually kill her. As he never actually had done.

All his killing-power would be outmatched. Having done what she was about to do and what, for him, would be so at the unthinkable extreme of what his daughter should do, she could and would outface him with it.

It might not even need words, though he might bawl and froth at her. She would take it. She, for once, would be like her mother. She would look at him and let her eyes speak. Well, come on then, hit me, if you're going to—at last. If this is what it takes. She would see his arm tense and his fist tighten. Come on then, if you dare. Her eyes would be like Lily's eyes, yet ferocious and unflinching: You won't dare.

And he wouldn't. It would all be as she foresaw. Having stepped so glaringly out of her own normal territory, she would see, more clearly than ever, how wretched and enraging was his own. And he would see her seeing it.

Poor man, poor prisoner. It would take most of her life and all of his before she was able to feel that. Poor prisoners, all of them. They clung to each other. They went down and up again, every day, in cages.

His arm would drop. She foresaw it. And his name was Armstrong.

What she hadn't foreseen was the other thing that would yet fire her defiance. Could she have defied him without it? Did he see it? Surely not. But perhaps he did. Perhaps it was what really broke him. Why was his daughter looking so changed, so charged, so aflame?

He wouldn't kill her. He wouldn't hit her. And he would never, to her knowledge, hit her mother again.

She would always remember it. The breeze blowing through the bus. The summer light outside. Her great act of daring? Or of kindness—for a shunned, marooned stranger? Or of freedom. Well yes, whatever else it was, she was plainly free to do this. And she could have had no idea of how weirdly, even distressingly free this man must have been feeling—in the service of his country as he was—to be able to get on a bus, to choose his own seat, to mix freely with other people.

She stood by him. He was still staring out of the window. On his head was a slightly comical wedge of a cap. He was suddenly aware of her presence. He turned and looked up. The whole bus must have been watching. He was a picture of surprise and confusion, which quickly turned into strange, scrambling duty. He half got up. She actually thought he was preparing to yield the entire seat to her. But she said—she hadn't known what she was going to say till she said it, 'May I?'

May I? Had she ever spoken such words? Had she ever been so formal and polite? She looked at the seat beside him, to make her meaning clear. He looked at it, then at her. She looked at him, for the first time, directly, and must have smiled. And she saw that his face, for all its sudden discomposure, was beautiful. Yes, beautiful. This was what she hadn't foreseen. This was the thing, of all things, that she hadn't expected, or even thought possible. The thing that fate alone supplied. That a man can just hit you. Not in *that* way. Just hit you.

She hadn't foreseen—or foreheard—the word 'beautiful' running so distinctly through her head, like a word from a foreign language. The word 'beautiful' was a word that went with 'woman', and then not so often. She didn't think she was beautiful. Only, perhaps, just a little bit prettier than Lily.

Was she beautiful that evening?

May I?

Now he was lifting his curled, joined black fingers to that cap. She was receiving a salute. She had never been saluted before. Then he smiled, a sudden relaxed smile, which lit his beauty.

'Why surely, ma'am. Surely. Make yourself at home.'

His voice was a purr. It came from somewhere she had never been. She was in unknown country. She had never been called 'ma'am' before. Why was everything so wonderfully courteous? And how had he come up, so naturally and magically, with that perfect wrong-way-round response?

They all must have been watching, from then on, for the next twenty minutes or so. And straining their ears. But there was the noise of the bus and the rippling breeze, and all those empty seats discreetly arranged around them!

When she got off, with the others, at Scarwood, everyone just looked at her and kept their distance—as if she herself had turned into a black man. Even Lily didn't know, immediately, what to say. Though what she wanted to say and would say, the next day, and what everyone else would want to say, at Dobson's—oh yes, it would be all round Dobson's—was: 'What did he *say*? And what did *you* say to him?' Nora Armstrong, sitting next to a black man on a bus. Bold as brass. And, clearly, they'd been speaking. Even smiling, laughing. Good God!

She could trust Lily, not to spread gossip. As if the gossip wouldn't spread anyway. It would be halfway round Scarwood in no time. She realised she had put Lily in a fix. But what could she do about it?

Within moments, after walking from the bus, she and Lily had parted, as usual, to go their separate ways to their separate homes. There had been a difficult silence, then Nora had said, 'Tata, Lil,' as if this day had been no different from any other. 'See yer tomorrer.' And Lily had said, 'Tata, Norrie.' But then said, 'Good luck.' Nora knew that Lily meant her father. Bless her. Lily knew that he'd be back from the pit by now. And it would get to his ears in no time. This was Scarwood.

So Lily would also be wanting to ask tomorrow, and perhaps it would be her first, anxious question: 'And what did your dad say, Norrie? Did he kill you?'

Well, obviously not. Dear Lily.

She parted from Lily, and walked on. But not, in fact, directly to her own home. She walked round a few corners, and then to where the houses ended and you could walk by open fields, the pithead in the distance. The fields had been recently harvested. There was just stubble. The light was golden and the stubble gleamed, and had a dry, baked smell. You couldn't smell the pit. The breeze was in the other direction.

On such an evening, it would have been good anyway to take this long-way-round walk, but she wanted to take it to make time pass, so that when she did return, her father would definitely know, it would have reached him. So it would be a simple matter—simple!—of just facing him. She wouldn't have to wait for a shock-wave to rock the house. And her mother would know too, and would back away. She knew it, foresaw it. For once, it would be that way round. Her mother would stay out of it and see what the upshot was. Well, her mother was going to thank her. Life was going to get less dangerous.

But she wanted to be alone with herself and the fields for another reason: to think of the thing that she hadn't foreseen. Thing? To think of *him*. She'd sat next to him and spoken to him, and wasn't that extraordinary enough? But she'd been hit, stunned. It can happen. She was feeling now the giddiness of it. She wanted to believe that it wasn't true. Yet she felt the simple truth of it. It had happened. She'd fallen for him. And why should she want to believe that it wasn't true?

Because she would never see him again. Of course not. So now—silly stupid girl—she would have to have, on top of anything else, the pain and pining and dreaming of it, for however long it took to get over it. And how long would that take? All her life? Don't be ridiculous.

But she'd fallen for him, been struck, which meant that, now, she could only love him. How? Well, at least she'd learned enough to know that *he* was unlikely to get killed any time soon. So she'd just have to mourn him—lose him—this way. And at least she knew that, while she loitered here by the stubble and he was still on the bus, on the way to Bessington, he must be thinking of her. How could he not be? He wouldn't forget her in a hurry, if he forgot her at all, this English girl—woman—who, somewhere in Nottinghamshire, had simply asked if *she* might sit next to *him*.

While he was still on the bus, she was still with him.

What had happened? Nothing and everything. Silly stupid girl. Did she think that, now, there could be anything more? No. What had happened had happened, such as it was. And she would never forget it and would have to keep it buried inside her.

But first she had to face—outface her father. And she knew that she *would* now, with all the more reason. With all that she had inside her now, she knew that she would defeat him, with all the more reason.

'What did he *say*, Norrie, what did he *say*?'

Well, he'd said that his name was Jeremiah and that he was from Alabama, and both words seemed as strange to her as each other.

'That's what my mama called me, ma'am. Pardon me, but I never knowed my daddy.'

Might she have said that she'd knowed hers? Only too well. And was his mama now thinking about him all the time and wondering where he was? *She* would have been, if she was his mama.

'But you can call me Jerry, ma'am. Though it's the name, these days, folks call a German. The enemy. I's not so sure it's such a good name.'

He smiled, a big smile, and held out his hand, a big hand, with long slender black fingers. He was quite tall. He was well built. His throat rose strongly, and blackly, from the collar of his uniform. And from the moment that it had first turned towards her, she'd thought that his face, his whole head was a marvel. It was so marvellously shaped that she'd thought it was like some piece of sculpture, placed there on his shoulders, and that it must be made of some remarkable black material all the way through. What a shocking thought to have had. But he'd never know.

She took his hand. It was more that his hand encased hers.

'Well, I guess now we're friends, ma'am, not enemies.'

And she said that her name was Nora. 'Nora' had no alternative ornate version like 'Jeremiah'. But he seemed to want to keep with his 'ma'am'. And she quite liked being called 'ma'am'. She said that she was Nora, from Scarwood, and felt her complete ordinariness. He would see what

Scarwood looked like, because it would be where she'd get off. She told him this, as if there might have been the option of just travelling on with him. She had no idea how Scarwood would compare with anywhere in Alabama. He would see that Scarwood was a coal mine, with houses. She felt ashamed.

'What did *you* say, Norrie? What did *you* say?'

Well, she must have found some way—some polite and careful way—of asking why he had been *there*, all by himself, at the bus station, why he was now on this bus. With her.

'Well, I's there, ma'am 'cause of Sergeant Hicks. I's there 'cause there's a store you has here called Boots. "Boots of Nottingham".' He said the ending of 'Nottingham' as if it had to do with pork. 'Sergeant Hicks tells me that Boots of Nottingham is the best store in England, and he sends me to Boots to get him some personal requirements 'cause he's too busy or lazy to get them hisself. But I thinks Sergeant Hicks is just playing a prank on me. He's just playing a prank on Jerry Dee. But when a prank's an order you have to obey.'

Jerry Dee didn't seem to have anything about him. Except his person.

'And—did you get them?'

'No, ma'am. I's afraid Boots had shortages. Or—pardon me—they didn't want to serve a stray like me, even though I speaks polite. I's afraid Sergeant Hicks is going to roast me. But I thinks he was only trying to put me in a spot in the first place. I's used to it. But, you see, I's thinking all along I had a half-day pass and it was my chance to see some of the sights. Of England. While I's here.'

'And did you see them?' It seemed the right thing to say.

'Well, ma'am, I guess the sights saw me.'

And she said that she worked in a factory, and how interesting was that? But she said it was a factory that made parachutes, since that had its connection. Then she thought that she shouldn't have said it, because it was careless talk.

But wasn't all this careless talk anyway? And everyone around them was struggling to hear.

'Well, I's afraid, ma'am, you can't make no nice parachute for me. I don't go up there, you see.' He raised his eyes to the roof of the bus. She saw again the marvel of his throat, his jaw. 'I aint one of them hero boys with wings. I just sticks to the ground and fixes the planes. Like all us strays. And that don't bother me.'

It seemed that he didn't think highly of himself, and didn't know that he—shone. She wanted to tell him—but how could she tell him politely?—that he shone. And it seemed that 'stray' was his word for, well, a black man. He was a 'stray'. And she supposed that he must feel like one, finding himself in Nottinghamshire instead of Alabama, and even having a hard time of it in Boots. She felt ashamed. But she was also feeling something else.

She'd never had a conversation like this in her life, though it was mainly a case of listening. But it had been her doing. And she was being struck, dazed.

And everyone was watching.

And all the talk that had been going round, careless or otherwise, must have been true. The RAF had pulled out of Bessington and the Americans had moved in. Not bombers, but transport planes, troop planes. They were flying them in, then flying them out again. Something was going on. And then there was the rumour that all the fliers and officers were whites, but all the ground crews and dogsbodies were blacks. Blacks! They had separate quarters.

'We just fixes up the planes and gets 'em ready. But I aint going to say no more, 'cause that's military business.' He looked solemn, he even drew the edge of his hand across his lovely throat. Then his face cracked. He smiled.

'I won't tell anyone,' she said. And she smiled herself.

'I knows you won't, ma'am. I knows I can trust you.'

It was as though they now shared a secret. And she was being captured, seized.

'And what else did he say, Norrie? And what did you say?'

'Well, Lil,' she found herself saying, 'careless talk . . .' It was a useful expression.

'Oh—come on, Norrie.'

Did Lily guess, could she tell? Couldn't she see it in her best friend's face?

'Some other time, Lil.'

'Norrie. You're not going to see him *again*, are you? You're not.'

Nora thought very carefully about her answer. She might have said all sorts of things. She might have been like Sergeant Hicks sending Jerry Dee to Boots. But she said very firmly (and truthfully), 'No, Lil, I'm not. And what are you *thinking*?'

And Lily might have guessed. But she didn't tell Lily that she would always think of *him* and see him in her head, trying to make his own beautiful head not fade, and see him in a dream or two. Would wonder about him and hope that he was all right.

'And your dad, Norrie? What about your dad?'

'Well, some other time too. But, as you can see, he didn't kill me, did he?'

And never would. And she would never use, even to Lily, that much-used phrase again.

It was not a long bus ride to Scarwood. Twenty minutes. Long enough to be captured. As the bus approached, she said again to her new-found friend, 'This is where I live. This is where I get off.' He looked out the window. What did he think? Were there slag heaps in Alabama? It was his moment to say something like, 'Well, now I know where to find you. I wonder if . . .' Was it possible? But he said nothing and she said, holding out her hand, 'It's been a pleasure to meet you, Jerry.' Where did she get all this dainty language from? Some hidden box inside her?

'Me too, ma'am. It's been a privilege.' It sounded more like 'purrvilige'. His hand enwrapped hers again. Did he squeeze it?

She said, 'Good luck, Jerry.' It was like saying that they would never meet again. He said, 'And good luck to you, ma'am. Nora. And thank you.'

Thank you?

Then, rejoining her friend Lily, who nonetheless kept a

little apart, she got off the bus, to find herself in Scarwood again, and to face the music.

Music? In Scarwood? But there was music, now, inside her. She was dancing to it.

And she would *talk* to him, of course, in her head. She would say to him, even that evening, 'Thank you, Jerry, thank you for helping me face my father. Thank you for being with me. Thank you for helping me get the better of the bastard. I couldn't have done it without you.'

She would go again, at other times, in the evening, while the fine August weather lasted, to the path by the fields. It was always hard to imagine that under the wheat fields were the seams of coal and the men with their helmet lamps. What was it about the stubble? Why did she want to stare at it? Of course, it was the colour of his uniform. With no one looking, she would burst, silly girl, into tears.

There were reasons, anyway, and they would arrive quite soon, why she never got round to saying much more to Lily, and why she had to push aside her—feelings. She would never see him again, but in any case he would soon be gone, sent elsewhere.

Have you heard? The Yanks have cleared out of Bessington. And worse things happened in war, far worse. People really did get killed. The RAF would soon be back, to carry on their bombing of Germany. And, putting two and two together, they would all know why the Americans had moved in so suddenly with their troop planes, then left just as quickly. There had been a big 'operation', in Holland. Thousands of men dropped by parachute.

So she and Lily, at Dobson's, had contributed.

But it seemed that this big operation had been a disaster. Certainly for the Alsop family. And certainly for Bert Alsop, who was there already, on the ground, in Holland. Having got there all the way from Africa. Well, he had seen a bit of the world. But he was killed, somewhere in Holland.

And Jerry Dee, all the way from Alabama, had seen a bit of the world. He had even been, one fine August day, to Boots in Mansfield.

So now she, Nora Armstrong, had to do what she could for her best friend, Lily, and for Lily's mother, and she knew that she must just keep quiet about her own—misery. Keep it to herself.

And should she be moping and pining anyway? For a man she'd met for twenty minutes on a bus?

When the war began, she and Lily had been thirteen, still at school. Now they were eighteen and the war still wasn't over. The big operation was supposed to have short-ened it. When the war started, all the miners shrugged and carried on, as they put it, 'as normal'. They would see nothing of the world. They saw nothing of it anyway, stuck down a pit. Blackouts? No problem. They could still use their lamps freely. Bombs, air-raid shelters? 'Well, pit roof might always fall on yer 'ed.' They carried on, with their famous cheery resignation. Oh yes?

The years between thirteen and eighteen were not good years to be the daughter and only child of a miner who hit his wife. Never mind that there was a war on. The women in the Armstrong household outnumbered their man two to one, but there was no denying who was in charge. When Nora began working, with Lily, at Dobson's, hand-ling all that fine white silk, she hardly ever thought of her father who at the same time would be not far away, under the ground, hacking out coal. But Lily must have thought all the time of her dad. Where was he? France? No, Holland.

How she wished that she could have done a swop, turned it all round. My dad for yours, Lil. Alf for Bert. Let my dad be the one who's gone. But her dad was the one who'd lived till 1984.

*

Greg said, 'Cup of tea?' He was still waiting, wondering. Might there still be some explosion?

Miners! They spent most of the time in the pit, or in the Spread Eagle, or lying, snoring in bed at night, worn out, and knocked out by beer. They didn't know how to be with anyone but themselves. Why should they?

It took a long time for her to find any pity, and then it seemed that it was all she could find. And they didn't want pity. Their place was the pit and they didn't want pity. When the war at last ended and the men—or some of them—returned, she could see that, every day, the miners came home like the men who came stumbling back from the war.

And if she'd ever been able to talk more to her Jerry, or Jeremiah (but she talked to him in her head), she might have been able to say that she, Nora Armstrong from Scarwood, was the daughter of a black man. Oh yes, a black man! Would this have amused him? Amazed him? Offended him?

But there'd been a time once, before they had the decency to put in the pit bath, when he'd come home black, a black man, like all of them, with oddly white, staring eyes. And then he'd have to sit in a tin tub in the kitchen, which her mother would have to fill and get ready for him, with the water the right heat. Woe betide her if she didn't. Woe betide her if the kitchen fire wasn't stoked. There was coal enough wasn't there?

He'd come home all black, in his blackened, sweat-damp pit clothes, and her mother would have to deal with them too. He'd want the kitchen to himself, he didn't want his wife to scrub him, but when he was done, he'd shout, 'Out!' And her mother would have to deal with the mess and mop the tiles.

Oh, I knowed my own daddy, Jerry. He hacked coal all day and scrubbed away the blackness from his skin. But he couldn't scrub away his hard black heart. Could she have said that?

He'd go into the kitchen black and come out white. She, his daughter, never witnessed the process in between. Of course not. It would have meant her seeing her father in the tub. And what would he have done then? Well, he would have killed her, wouldn't he? But he'd have had to jump out of the tub first, wouldn't he? And then she would have truly seen her father, all white and naked or all black and naked, whichever it was.

She thought that Jerry might have laughed. She herself would come to laugh, but only to herself, at the thought that would have once been so scary. Alf Armstrong hopping, naked, round the kitchen, about to slay his daughter.

When he was dying, a bag of bones, the thought of it (though not while Greg was looking) made her weep.

She and Greg had watched the news. A battle was going on. The police, hundreds of them, some of them on horses, were charging and chasing the miners. There were large numbers of miners too. But the police had the horses, the helmets, shields and sticks. The miners were being overpowered, broken up. They ran, then stopped to throw things and yell. Sometimes they surged back, but the police thrust their shields against them and used their sticks. There were miners lying or sitting on the ground, injured. There were police on the ground too. The horses were frightening. It was mayhem, savage.

Then Greg had said that thing about her father not being around to see it. And of course he was right and it was a decent thought. Dear Greg. But all she could muster now was the stubborn pity. Stuck down a mine, never set free, even in the war. Not a hero, though some thought miners were heroes now, fighting a war. Greg probably thought so.

She'd never told Greg what a terrible man her father had once been. An absurd sense of betrayal still gripped her.

And now he was dead, it would seem even more a betrayal, like going behind an ever-turned back. The last scrap of undeserved loyalty she'd pay him.

She'd never told Greg how her mother, who'd died first (and by how many years had her life been shortened?), bore the bruises and kept her own mouth shut. Greg, she thought, had always wanted to think, in his university lecturer's way, that having married a miner's daughter was some kind of badge of honour, a credential. Well, let him think it.

They, she and Greg, had been set free. Yes, after the war, they were still just about young enough to be set free, and know it.

She'd never told Greg lots of things.

But her mind had been floating away and she really hadn't been thinking, even as they'd watched the miners being chased and rounded up, of her father. She'd been thinking of all the other scenes like this, on the telly, that she and Greg, in their time, had seen. Charging police, beatings, things being set on fire. Rage.

It was long, long ago, but, oh, how sometimes she could still ridiculously miss him and wonder where he was. And, oh, how sometimes she was tempted to say to Greg, who would never understand, that once long ago, walking up the aisle of a bus—it wasn't really much to do, sitting next to a man and even asking first if she might—she had done, in the language of the time, her bit. Never mind all those white silk parachutes, she had done her bit.

X

PALACE

PALACE

'Crystal Palace'. It had become the name of a loosely defined region of south London and, more officially, of a football team, in those days never getting far up a thing called the Third Division. 'Third Division'—it was like 'third class', but nobody said so. And who could ever have given to a football team the name of something out of fairyland?

But you didn't think about it as you watched the boys out there on the pitch, doing their best against Southend, you didn't think it was strange that they were collectively known as 'Crystal Palace' or, for short, just 'Palace'. You didn't think it was odd to say, 'I live in Crystal Palace.' You might have said 'Penge' or 'Norwood'. And how exciting were those names?

But where was it, this fabled and glittering Crystal Palace? Nowhere. It was not to be seen. The whole point of it, or so it seemed to me as a kid, was that it *had* been there, but it was gone. Though how could any 'crystal palace' ever have been real in the first place?

But my dad and mum could remember it, the real thing, and, one evening, they let me know it, in their different ways. It was winter, or late autumn. It was dark outside. The fire was lit in the hearth. Yes, a real coal fire. The tiles of the fire surround were a glinting honey-brown. We lived in Ballantyne Road, SE19. I'm pretty sure it was November—it would have been appropriate. And I would have been eleven. My little sister, Jean, would already have been tucked up in bed. And I think it was a Monday, as on the preceding Saturday 'Palace' had lost—yet again—to Queens Park Rangers, and this had made my dad unhappy. His unhappiness had carried over to Monday, even to Monday evening, and Mondays were not the greatest of days anyway.

Unhappiness? Perhaps a better word might be 'rancour'— a word I didn't have then. My dad had a capacity for rancour. Not so much unhappiness, but a cultivated and combative sense of injustice. I had watched, with him, the slaughtering by QPR, but I was just a small boy and could be more even-tempered about it.

I sometimes called him 'my old man'. Not to his face, of course, or in his hearing, but with my school mates. We had a thing going about calling our fathers 'my old man'. That November night, he would still have been in his late thirties, but in my head, and he never knew it, he was 'my old man'.

He worked in the office at the railway yards in Selhurst. He did something to do with trains. He'd never been an engine-driver or signalman or anything that might have fascinated a small boy, but he was 'in railways'. At some point in my early years, which he must have judged finely, he started to take me to watch Palace play at home. There was no question that this was going to happen one day and that I'd have no say in it. My mum would have seen it coming, too, and knew that she'd have no say, either. My little sister, Jean, wouldn't have had much say in anything, because she would have then been only about four.

I became a Palace supporter. I stood beside my dad and watched Palace, more often than not, get thrashed. Their home ground was called Selhurst Park. 'Park' was as mysterious as 'Palace'. There was nothing 'park' about it. It was a Third Division football stadium—a big damp draughty shed. But what's in a name? Why weren't Palace called Selhurst United or even Selhurst Wanderers? Who's ever heard of Selhurst, anyway?

'My old man'. It's a complicated expression. It's not derogatory, but nor should it be used carelessly. Even now, in my head, I can call him 'my old man', and with more exactness, because he became old, and then he died. He's gone now, like the Crystal Palace, but he was my old man.

He wasn't an old man that night. But there were lots of still quite young men then who seemed to topple readily into being old men. They lingered on the edge of it, as if it were a tempting choice. And he smoked a pipe, which was like an instant claiming of seniority. All that fuss of filling it and lighting it, then, later, tapping out the ash, all that gesticulating that could go with holding the thing. Not to mention the great puffs of smoke. No wonder he worked on the railways.

Plenty of men who weren't old smoked pipes in those days, it was nothing unusual. What happened to all those pipes of the 1950s? Was there a collection one day, like an amnesty? What happened to all those high-street tobacconists, little temples some of them, where you could buy loose pipe-tobacco weighed out on a pair of scales?

My old man.

In the war, since he worked on the railways, he'd been

deemed 'reserved occupation'. So he (and my mum) only had to live through the Blitz. I don't know what he did. He kept the trains running, I suppose, despite all the bomb damage. Quite important stuff. But he'd never 'fought', and this, I've always thought, had left him with a lasting grievance, or a general disposition to nurse grievances. Bursts of 'fighting-talk'. Swearing at football matches (if only my mum could have heard). This was my never-spoken theory anyway.

But my old man was the one for theories. He made no bones about his affiliations, persuasions and understandings of the world. He had no time for Churchill. Churchill's game was to screw the workers. Yes, of course, it was bloody well right that we'd stood up to Hitler (Churchill would have agreed), but it was the Russians who'd really won the war and saved our skins, not the bloody Yanks, who'd only put us in debt for ever.

With all such stuff, quite a lot of business with his pipe.

He was not a communist or a revolutionary, he was just, not so far beneath his sometimes quite gentle, pipe-smoking surface, a stew of gripes and grouses. You could see it starting to bubble. He'd light his pipe and off he'd go. I was too young to know, much of the time, what on earth he was talking about, but not too young—it sounds both precocious and harsh—to realise that, quite often, nor did he.

But I had to listen. Small as I was, I could tell that, for all his force of opinion, he was only getting himself into furious tangles. He did it all the time. He started and he couldn't stop. He went off on tangents. He couldn't keep to an argument. He contradicted himself. I could see the demons taking hold, and wanted to intercept them, but didn't know how.

'At least the bloody Yanks got it right about royalty. They told our lot where to get off ages ago, didn't they? About time we did the same. Bloody royal family.'

This was a recurring theme. It was as if at some time the royal family had all personally insulted him. Yet he supported a football team called 'Palace'. Not so long before he took me to my first match there had been a Coronation. There was a feeling in the air—I can just about remember it—that dark days were over. Our new young queen had been driven to be crowned, in a picture-book golden coach.

When I went with him, those first times, to 'the Park', I quickly understood that going to the footie offered him a respite from his scatter-shot resentments—or gave them a focus. 'Where did they get this bloody ref from?' It suited him to support an underdog team. It wouldn't really have pleased him if Palace had got too victorious.

But how could a team called Palace ever be underdogs?

The real Crystal Palace was no longer there. There was only—visible from Selhurst Park—the long ridge of the hill where once it had stood. The ghost of the Crystal Palace looked down on the football team. What you could see, very plainly, up on the hill, was a newly erected TV mast, a sort of slender Eiffel Tower and a symbol of its age, the 1950s, as once, I came to learn, the Crystal Palace had been, of its age, a century before.

You couldn't have made it up, the story of the Crystal Palace. It was a real story, but, appropriately enough, a kind of fairy tale. There had been proposed by Queen Victoria, or by those who counselled her, that there should be a Great Exhibition—a Great Exhibition of Great Britain and her Empire and of all associated works and wonders. Had there even been such a conceited idea? And this exhibition needed to be housed. So there was duly constructed in Hyde Park a building of astonishing design, a wonder, in itself, of girders and glass, called the Crystal Palace. Where else, other than in Wonderland, was there ever such a thing?

The Exhibition took place and was the marvel of all.

Then it finished, and there was the question: What to do with the Crystal Palace? Leave it there, taking up room in Hyde Park? Perhaps not. Demolish it and dispose of it? Surely not—and how? The answer was to take it down, piece by enormous piece, and transport it to be re-erected on a hilltop in south London.

These Victorians knew how to do things. Look around you, in south London, in the 1950s, and a great deal of what you saw, though the Victorians themselves had disappeared, was still 'Victorian'. Houses, streets. Railway lines, railway bridges, railway tunnels—why should I think of them? The Victorians had built the fabric of the world in which you stood. There it still was, despite two wars, and, whatever you thought of the Victorians—weren't they those pompous, stuffy people who thought that even table legs were rude?—you had to be thankful that they'd built things to last.

Except, in November 1936, the Crystal Palace, getting on for being a hundred years old, had burnt down.

This was the subject of my dad's particular rant that evening, and I don't know what had sparked it off. Wrong expression. I was later to understand that what had caused the Crystal Palace to burn to the ground had long been a matter of speculation, and my dad was bound to deliver his view at some point. But, after two decades, it was generally agreed that it had simply caught fire. It can happen with buildings, even immense and historically unique ones. They just catch fire.

I'm pretty sure it was November 1956. Our own fire was aglow. My dad lit his pipe, and off he went. And I soon had the thought: Why did the Crystal Palace catch fire? Because some fool of a pipe smoker had dropped an unextinguished match.

But my dad vigorously shook out his own match. He liked to do this with some assertion. It was a sort of pay-attention sign that he was going to say something. He became 'my old man'.

'Obvious, wasn't it? Obvious all along. It was Mosley's gang, of course it was. The bloody blackshirts. They wanted to create a scare. They wanted to make out it was the Jews or the commies that had done it. It was their version of the Reichstag fire. They wanted to drive us all into the arms of Adolf. That was the way things were going anyway, wasn't it? Look at that Edward and that Mrs What-was-her-name—Mrs Simpson. They were a fishy pair all along, if you ask me. But it was Mosley and his boys. And look where it got them—nowhere.'

I was eleven years old. I knew some things, but not a lot, and I didn't know, as usual, most of what my dad was on about. Who was Mrs Simpson? As for the 'Reichstag'—if I'd even heard the word correctly—what the hell was that? What my dad had launched into must have been for my benefit, because my mum must surely have heard it all before. In fact, that night, she did something, very much for my benefit, that she'd quite often do when my dad sounded off. She would somehow catch my sideways attention, then raise her eyebrows—very slightly, but just enough—and at the same time give me the tiniest twist of a smile.

She was very good at this, and my dad didn't notice it, because when he held forth, he tended to look peculiarly into the air. No, it was not for my mum's benefit or even my own that he pronounced, but mainly for the benefit of an appreciative and enlightened audience that wasn't there.

But I got my dad's gist. The Crystal Palace had been deliberately set on fire for some dubious purpose. A man called Mosley had something to do with it, and possibly a woman called Mrs Simpson. But the most striking thing was that when my dad spoke there was no hint of his personal connection—that is, that he might have witnessed this spectacular event himself. Wasn't it likely? It would have been up the road. And if he had, wouldn't it have been, before it was anything else, just—a spectacular event? And if you'd been there, wouldn't it have been the first thing you'd have wanted to say? I was there!

I would.

So perhaps he just wasn't there. In any case, in his account there was no scene-painting, no sense of simple amazement. It was all about some devious plot. Nor was there any suggestion of sorrow. The Crystal Palace was *gone*. That great building that had stood there, all those decades, up on the hill, was no more.

In fact, my dad seemed not unpleased that the Crystal Palace had burnt down, and he finally came out with it.

'But if you ask me, I never liked the bloody thing in the first place. Great monstrosity. Great bloody monument to Queen Victoria.'

He seemed to have forgotten Mosley and his men. There was another target, another culprit. It was all down to Queen Victoria. I was only eleven, but I had come to see that my father lived in a world of all-pervasive conspiracy. He couldn't exist without it.

And things went round in their ensnaring circles.

'Bloody King Edward and Mrs What's-her-face. Well, they nearly sold us right down the river, didn't they?'

Then he knocked the ash from his pipe and said that he

was going to the Greene Man. This could happen. A certain confused and inconclusive point would be reached and my old man would go to the Greene Man.

My mum was a very tolerant woman, and she was very sensitive and diplomatic when dealing with me, her only son, in the context of her husband. When he declaimed, she would give me those sly yet tender looks. They were only looks, not conversations. I would come to understand that my mum's real conversations would be with my sister—when Jean was old enough. I think that when my mum's second child came along in the form of a girl, it was to my mum's great relief and solace about the future of her marriage.

But that night, and soon after my dad's departure for the Greene Man, I got a conversation from my mum—or I listened to what she had to say. I think she had decided that, whether I was old enough or not—and I wasn't really old enough—the time had come.

I had the feeling that she was taking me secretly aside. As she spoke, she glanced now and then in the direction of the front door, as if my dad might at any moment return, having decided not to confer with the Greene Man. Or perhaps be crouching in the front porch—it had all been a ruse—his ear pressed tightly to the letter box.

'You see, Dickie,' she said, 'I was there with him. I was standing, watching, arm in arm with him, when it burnt down.'

She had at once made something very clear that had not been clear. She was obviously talking, as my dad had been, about the historical event—'The Great Crystal Palace Fire'—but the little words that touched me were 'arm in arm'. It was as if my mother had slipped her own arm into mine.

'We were both there. You wouldn't have known it, would you?' She must have read my eleven-year-old thought. 'But we were. November 1936. Coats and scarves, but we didn't need them, Dickie, because of the heat. Goodness me, the *heat*! We were both there, watching. So were thousands of other people. You could have seen it for miles and miles around. So we had to be there, didn't we? We lived just down the hill. But people were flocking from miles and miles around.'

Coming from my mum's lips was everything that had not come from my dad's. She drew a sigh—or, rather, a necessary, steadying intake of breath. She might, still, have backed out of what she was about to say. It suddenly seemed to me, a small boy, that my mother wanted somehow to apologise to me for my father. What a thing. She had married him.

But 'apologise' was not the right word.

I'd never heard her draw breath or drag words from inside her in this way before. And never would again. Ahead lay a critical passage of years. Jean would become her confidante—her provisional, then her full confidante. Then I would be stuck with my dad. But that would be a wrong and cruel way of putting it, and it was not what my mum wished me to think.

I already went, with my old man, to watch the football. One day, when I was of age, I would go with him, also, to the Greene Man. I could see it coming, so could my mum. My first ritual pint with my father. And my mum would have Jean. There are things that are so hard to get out of.

What my mother said to me I shall never forget.

'You see, Dickie, always understand this. I want you always to understand this. I love him. I love him, anyway. It's how it is. I simply love him.'

What a thing for her to say to me, and at an age before I was truly ready for it. But she was seizing her moment. I was only eleven, but I had my first premonition that time is this stuff that slips away. Had my dad been a different man, a different creature, in 1936, before the war?

A simple thing to say—she herself had said 'simply'—but

not simple at all. I would have understood it, I would not have thought it a contradiction, if with her next breath she'd said, 'Your bloody father!'

But she said again, 'We were both there!' And I could *see* her remembering. I could see a warmth coming into her face, as if I were looking at a woman who was no longer looking at me, but at a great astonishing mass of flames.

'You see, Dickie, it was all—so extraordinary. The whole thing was just—burning down! Great bits of it were falling and crashing down. The police were keeping people back. We stood there and we watched it all. But I want to tell you something, I want you to know it. As we stood there, your dad and me, we just suddenly started *laughing*! We just started to laugh! It wasn't for long, and it wasn't what we should have done, was it? The Crystal Palace was burning down right in front of us, it should have been a warning to us all, but we just started laughing!

'And do you know why we started laughing, Dickie? Well, I'll tell you. It was because we were young and alive and happy. A great building going up in flames before our eyes—well it only made us all the more aware of it.

'I want you to know this, Dickie. I want you to remember it. Your dad and me, when the Crystal Palace was burning down, we just started laughing.'

And I did remember it. I do remember it. As if I was there.

What had I done—though I couldn't have had this thought at the time—to deserve such a mother? Who could tell me such a thing. Who could put such a picture in my mind. And what fools men are, going off to football matches and just shouting—shouting their heads off, shouting all the same things as each other.

'It was a night to remember, you see, Dickie. That's what everyone said: "a night to remember". For your dad and me it was a night to remember in more ways than one.'

When she said this, she looked into some space above me, as if she might have been talking to a son twice my age.

And my mum has gone now, too. But I'll always remember her, as she was that night—our little gesture of a fire flickering in the hearth—when my old man went to the Greene Man.

'You see, your dad, the very next day—he was very quick, he didn't waste any time—made sure that he and I got engaged. I mean, Dickie, that we would get married. That's how it happened. That's what the Crystal Palace catching fire did for us. So I suppose we should be grateful.

'But I'm sorry too. I mean, I'm sorry that it burnt down. It didn't have to, did it? It was terrible. It was sad. Your dad didn't seem to mind, did he? Your dad seemed to be saying, "Good riddance." But I think he was sorry too, in his own way. Oh, I think so. It had been there all those years, and then it was gone.

'And I'm sorry you never saw it, Dickie. I mean, before it burnt down. I suppose they'd have bombed it to bits in the war anyway, but I'm sorry you never saw it. It was one of those things that could make you feel: As long as it's still there . . .

'But don't worry, Dickie. And don't you worry about all that claptrap your dad spouts. There's always some old building still left standing somewhere to look at. There's always the Tower of London.'

XI

BRUISES

BRUISES

'The quiet ones are the worst.' I've never understood that expression. What's wrong with quiet? Surely it's the noisy ones who are the worst. Surely it's noise, generally, that there's too much of.

I don't like noise. I had enough noise in the Hussars. But they say the quiet ones are the worst. If everything's quiet, then it means a bomb will go off. You can't win.

It seemed to be the issue when Shirley kicked me out. My quietness, I mean. I don't mean Shirley literally kicked me out. There was no kicking. Shirley didn't kick me, I didn't kick her. It wasn't a case of the 'domestic violence' you hear about. It was my quietness that started it. Shirley could see that I'd gone into myself. That's what I used to do in those days—I'd go into myself.

Shirley said, 'You never talk, you never say things.' I think what she meant was that I wasn't much fun any more. I'd agree with that. If I ever had been, I wasn't any more, I'd stopped being fun. I'd gone into myself, like a worm into a hole. I think she meant that she'd found out at last—and I'm surprised it took her so long—that she'd hooked up with a sort of invalid.

I said to her once, and it was all I ever said on the subject, 'I was in the Hussars in Iraq, Shirl.'

'What's a Hussar?'

'I've no idea, Shirl, but I was one.'

When Shirl started to go for me, I said, 'Don't raise your voice.'

'I'm not raising my voice.'

'You are.'

She wasn't shouting, she'd just raised her voice, but I was afraid she might start shouting, and then things would get noisy. I'd never raised my voice at Shirley. I hadn't been with her for so long, but it was longer than with anyone else. I'd never shouted at her or done anything worse. I'd never raised a finger, let alone my voice. But now, it seemed, I'd gone too quiet.

She said, 'Two, three nights a week, you're not even here. Even when you're here, you're not here.'

I didn't deny it. I thought: All this is fair enough and I had it coming. That's a good expression: I had it coming. You had it coming. He, she or they had it coming. We all have it coming.

Shirley was a good woman. There was a time when with Shirl I'd let myself think: Now I'm home, this is home. A crap neighbourhood, but it was home. She worked mornings in a nursery school. Then she'd work afternoons in a coffee place, one of those kiosks close to the Tube station. Sometimes I'd be passing by and I'd go to the kiosk and order a coffee and pretend I didn't know her, and see how long she'd pretend, too, that she didn't know me. That we were complete strangers. Which of us would blink first? Laugh first?

Yes, for a while we had fun. We'd laugh. Laughter's a kind of noise. Kids in a nursery school must make a lot of noise. I wondered if Shirley ever told them to shut up, just to shut up.

I worked as an orderly in a mental hospital, the Langston. It was work I could get, work I could do. It could sometimes get noisy at the Langston, but the strange thing was, I didn't mind it. I never found the Langston scary or creepy.

It takes one to recognise another, maybe. In and out of a mental hospital every day, sometimes night shifts, too. But it didn't bother me, I didn't find it strange.

Shirley said, 'Why do you work in that place?'

'It's a job, Shirl. It pays the rent. It doesn't bother me. Does it bother you?'

Shirley didn't answer that, but she looked at me. She looked at me a bit like when she was serving me a coffee and pretending not to know me. But she wasn't getting ready to laugh.

Shirley used to wear a red dress, a tight red dress. I mean, not all the time. It wasn't an all-the-time dress. It was like Shirley flying her special flag. She certainly didn't wear it to the nursery school. Then there'd have been some noise. I said, 'I like you in that dress, Shirl. It's your colour.' She could tell I meant a bit more than that. 'I like you in that dress and I like you when you're not in it.'

Yes, we used to have some fun, but then I went into myself. I thought I wouldn't. I'd been starting to think I never would again. But I did.

Some people say that red is a 'loud' colour. But how can that be? How can any colour make a noise? 'Red rag to a bull'. 'Seeing red'. I've never understood those expressions, either. Why red is the colour of anger. I just told Shirley that I liked her in her red dress. So she wore it quite a lot.

But then one day, when I'd gone into myself, I said, 'Don't you ever get tired of that red dress, Shirl?' It wasn't right, it wasn't fair to say that. And she kept wearing it anyway, she kept wearing it even more after that. It troubled me. But I kept quiet, I didn't say anything. A colour is just a colour.

And now she was saying to me, 'Even when you're here, you're not here.'

Well, that might have needed some thinking about. But I didn't deny it, I understood it. I didn't ask her what she meant. I might have said that she was spot-on.

I said, 'Are you chucking me out, Shirl?' I said it quietly, I wasn't arguing. I wasn't lifting a finger. 'I want to be clear about it. Are you chucking me out? I'm not chucking *you* out. But we share the rent on this place. Are you chucking me out?'

I could see that she was getting fired up, like she might, instead of saying things, start throwing things around. She wouldn't hit me, I wouldn't hit her, but she might start throwing things, even throwing them at me. I could see that things were starting to get tricky.

I said, 'Yes or no, Shirl?'

She made a sound, through her teeth, a sort of savage sound. She'd said that I never talked, but now it seemed that she was the one who couldn't get the words out.

'Yes or no.'

'Yes.'

Then she really raised her voice.

At the Langston it's sometimes part of my job to 'restrain' a patient. Nobody told me it might be part of my job, I was never trained. On the other hand, I *was* trained. I think they looked at me and thought: He'll be all right for the job.

She really raised her voice. 'Yes! Yes I am! And while you're at it, you can go to hell!'

That was telling me.

I said, 'Okay, Shirl. Fair enough. It's been nice knowing you.'

I didn't raise my voice. But I know when I'm being told. I know when I'm not wanted. There comes a point when you know things.

So I got my zip-up jacket and I walked out the door. I didn't slam it. I just walked out. It was dark and damp and chilly.

*

What was I going to do next? Did I have a plan? Search me. On the other hand, it was obvious. I walked to where I'd been going those two or three nights a week that Shirl had talked about. She'd chucked me out, but on the other hand nothing had changed. I walked to the Blue Anchor. We lived in an area of pretty rough pubs, but the Blue Anchor was the roughest of the lot. That's why I went there. I'd never have gone there with Shirl. It was the sort of pub where you only ever saw men hanging out. And most of them pretty rough. And I was one of them.

A tricky patient at the hospital, a noisy one? No problem. I hardly ever had to use force. That's because they could see that I could. Otherwise, at the Langston they liked to keep things polite. You weren't even supposed to say 'mental' hospital—it was 'psychiatric' hospital. In the old days they used to call such places 'asylums', they used to call the ones inside 'lunatics'. Now it was 'patients', not even 'inmates'.

But I wasn't bothered. If they were inmates, poor bastards, I was an outmate. I was a mate anyway. I wasn't trained in psychiatry, but I'd say, 'Take it easy, mate. Keep a lid on it.'

Shirley knew about me working at the Langston, but she'd never been in it. Why should she? And she knew about me going to the Anchor. Clearly. But she'd never been in the Anchor, either.

The place I'd go to that Shirley never knew about, and still doesn't, was the Catholic church, St Mark's, on Winterton Road. Big red-brick place, nearly always empty. I used to pop in there sometimes on my way back from my shift. The coffee kiosk usually, but sometimes, by a different route, the Catholic church. I'm not a Catholic. My dad was in Northern Ireland. King's Hussars. I'm not a church-goer, but if you go into a church and sit quietly, they can't kick you out.

That's what I'd do sometimes, just sit there quietly. I'd see those things like cupboards along the side—the confessionals—and I'd sometimes think: I wish I could do that, just for the hell of it. No, I don't mean that. Just for the peace and quiet of it, the talking in whispers, with someone you don't know and can't even see.

'Forgive me, father, for I have sinned . . .'

'And what was your sin?'

'The sin of murder, father. But I was in the Army and in another country, and it was a few years ago now.'

If you went into one of those cupboards and you weren't a Catholic, or even anything, could they stop you? How would they know?

But that night when Shirley chucked me out I didn't go to the Catholic church, I went to the Blue Anchor. The barman knew me. I mean, he didn't know me, but he'd seen me quite a few times already, and he knew my game. I didn't want any chatty talk. I just wanted to sit quietly with my drink, and always at the bar, if there was a space. On a stool at the bar, even though I didn't want any chatty talk with the barman. What was wrong with that? It was a pub.

Barman? Landlord too, I'd guess. Both. It was his place and he ran it. Not much of a place, but the best he could get. And he was in charge, no doubt about it. He had to be. Big hefty bastard too. You wouldn't want to mess. Or most wouldn't.

One night I'd come back from the pub with my face 'all mashed up'. At least, that's what Shirley said. It was just a few scrapes. 'Your face is all mashed up.'

'It's nothing, Shirl. Just a bit of bother.'

She said, 'What the hell's going on? This has got to stop.'

True. She never said a truer thing. If you want to cure yourself of something, if you want to pull yourself out of it, you stop it. Simple.

How much dope-dealing was going on at the Anchor? Search me. Quite a lot. But it wasn't my business. It wasn't my problem. It wasn't my poison.

That night, I went down to the Anchor again and sat at the bar. There was a space and I took up as much of it as possible. Elbows out, shoulders spread, and I'm not a small man. Always at the bar. Sit at the bar and mean it. So others at the bar, getting their drinks, have to reach round you or over you, or perhaps jog into you just as you're lifting your pint to your mouth.

So then I could say, 'Excuse me!'

'Excuse you what?'

'I'm sitting here.'

'You're sitting there, are you?'

And then, if I had anything to do with it, it might all kick off. But the barman would see that I hadn't started it, that it had nothing to do with me. I was just someone who'd been knocked into while sitting quietly with a drink. Oh yeah?

And, that night, he must have seen that I really meant business. So I had it coming. He'd seen me before, he'd seen my kind before. And he had the look, himself, of someone who'd done time. I mean, not just behind a bar. Behind *bars*, maybe. In the Army. In a boxing ring. For all I knew, in the Langston loony-bin.

You have to know about it, you have to know about being in a fight, before you go looking for one. My dad was in the Army too. He loved it. He was a bully. He was over there in Belfast. He made me follow in the family tradition.

The barman saw me trying it on again. This time I really meant business. He'd seen it in my face.

'Excuse me!' Spilt beer all over his bar, but nothing to do with me.

This time it was really going to blow up. Except, before it began, it was all over. Before I knew it, that barman had come round from behind the bar, opening and shutting his flap. Before I knew it, he was standing behind me, and everyone else was standing back. Before I knew it, his hands were on my arms, and not just on them, but clamping them hard against my sides so I couldn't move them, and he was lifting me up—just lifting me up, easy-peasy—off my stool, so my legs were dangling and my feet weren't even touching the ground.

And they never did. My God, he had some strength. Then he was carrying me, like I was a piece of broken furniture, arms clamped, feet not touching anything, to the door. He kicked open the door, still holding me, and then we were out on the pavement. There was traffic and lights. Passers-by. Well, they had something to pass by. Only then did he put me down, only then was I standing on my own two feet again, but he still had my arms tight against me, and he was twisting me round, like some kind of pole. All, apparently, so I'd be facing in the right direction.

He said, 'Now you walk. Okay? You walk. You walk in that direction.' He let go of my arms so, in case I hadn't got the message, he could point the way, but my arms still stuck to my sides. 'You walk. And you keep on walking till you get to hell.'

That was telling me.

Why he thought that hell was in that particular direction, I'll never know. There were two possible directions along the pavement, but he'd twirled me round and he'd chosen that one.

I might have said to him, 'You don't have to do this. I've already been told to go to hell this evening.' Or I might have said, 'You don't have to tell me to go to hell, I've already been there.' But I didn't say either of those things. I'm a quiet man. I don't like noise. And I walked. I walked with my arms still pinned to my sides. I walked like a clockwork man who'd just been wound up.

And it happened to be in the direction I'd come from. Back to where I lived, or thought I'd lived. Back to where I'd shut the door, without slamming it, on Shirl, then walked to the pub.

And it happened to be not in the direction of hell.

Some time after all this was over, it occurred to me that the other direction would have been my way to work, to the Langston. It would have been a long walk—I took the Tube to work, several stops—but if the barman had pointed me in that direction, I think I would have kept on walking, just as he'd told me, till I got to the Langston. And when I got there, I might have said, 'It's all right—I work here. But now I'm thinking of staying. I've got nowhere else to go. Will you let me in?'

If you want to cure yourself of something, you stop it. Fair enough. I might have said to that barman as he parked me on the pavement, 'This isn't the first time I've been chucked out this evening.'

But I walked. I walked in the direction he pointed out to me. And I didn't stop till I got to the door that I hadn't slammed behind me. And I knocked. It was quite hard to knock, because my arms still wanted to stay by my sides.

Shirley opened the door. Had she been expecting this? I'll never know. I looked at her. I said, 'I hope you didn't mean it, Shirl, I hope you didn't mean it, because I've come back.'

She looked at me. She looked at me for quite a long

while, until I even thought: Does she recognise me? But then she said, no, she hadn't meant it. And I said I hadn't meant it either, whatever it was I'd meant or not meant. And she let me in.

Home is where they let you in. I might have been in a police cell, with my face really mashed up. Serve me right. I might have been in the Langston and not getting paid for it. Wasn't I lucky? Wasn't I lucky that the barman had pointed me in the wrong direction for hell? How did he do it? How did he make such a basic mistake?

Shirley let me in. Then things happened fast. They'd already happened fast. I know that things can happen fast. Before you know it, they've already happened. I know all about that.

And before we knew it, Shirl and I weren't standing up any more, looking at each other like strangers. Our feet weren't touching the ground and we were in another, more friendly situation, where we generally remained all night.

And I'd swear now, looking back, that it was that night that, by hook or by crook or by complete accident, that our first one—Martin (it was Shirley's dad's name)—got conceived. It was something else that happened that night.

One day I might tell Martin—he's three years old now and he has a little sister, Jessie—how it happened, how *he* happened. But maybe that wouldn't be such a great idea. I might just say to him, 'Promise me one thing, Mart—never join the Army.' And I'll never know if Shirley had the same hunch as me, or even some kind of direct knowledge. That it was that night. I've never asked, she's never said. But she had a job in a nursery school. I should have got the message, I should have seen it coming.

It was only in the morning that she said, looking at me in the daylight, 'What the hell's happened? What the hell's going on? You've got big bruises on both your arms.'

I never went back to the Blue Anchor again. Surprise, surprise. That barman must have thought that, sure enough, he'd sent me to the right place. And, so far—and it's been a long time now and I have two kids—I've never gone back into myself like I used to. I've never gone back to that place.

My God, he must have had some strength, some arms. I wish I'd known his name. One day Shirl told me that she'd never known her dad. She'd just known—from her mum—that his name was Martin.

I might have said to Shirl but I didn't, 'I knew my dad, and I knew his name. Worse luck.'

But I said to her as she looked at the bruises, 'Yes, I noticed them too. I don't think it was something *you* did, was it, Shirl? I'll tell you all about it later. But I've got to get to work. I'll tell you all about it later.'

XII

Passport

Passport

Some two years ago, Anna-Maria Anderson, then approaching her eightieth birthday, had renewed her passport. Her existing one was about to expire. She couldn't remember, now, how this had come to her attention. When had she last used her passport? What on earth did she need a new one for? Was she planning on going anywhere?

Nonetheless, she felt she must renew it, out of a kind of duty. She had maintained a passport since—well, she couldn't remember. A valid passport was one of those things you simply had to have, as you should always have, or so she'd once believed, a good winter coat. It was a form of personal reinforcement, it announced you to the world.

It *offered* you the world. Not to have such a facility was, in a way, not to exist. Or, turning it round, having it was like having a faithful friend. Was she simply going to let her companion die?

So she had renewed it, for another ten years. And so she must have had the fleeting thought: Will I expire before my new passport does or will it expire before me?

Now she sat, very early on an October morning, on the chair before her bureau, examining her passport. She had taken it from the drawer where for two years—she had checked that it was a little over two years—it had rested in largely undisturbed darkness. It still looked, unlike herself, brand-new.

She had forgotten how old she was. It was her birthday. She knew that her birthday was 10th October. But she couldn't be sure if she was going to be eighty-one or eighty-two. Did it matter? Perhaps not. But as she'd lain awake in the early hours of this special day, she'd been aware that she didn't know how many years she'd attained, and though no one else need know or care about this, nor, really, need she, yet it was something of a failure. What had things come to?

Being awake in the small hours was nothing unusual. It was not excitement at her incipient birthday. It was a condition of age. She knew this all too well. But then the exact question of her age had assailed her. Was it eighty-one or eighty-two? Or possibly even eighty-three?

She remembered her passport. It was a sort of flash of inspiration. Her passport would tell her! And then a kind of birthday giddiness had enveloped her. She was visited for a moment, uncannily, by a memory, from long ago, of being up and out of bed early, when she'd been very small. Had it been her birthday? It was so long ago that it was perhaps before she *had* a memory. So had it really been her? Then the little hallucination had disappeared.

Where was her passport? It was in the drawer in the bureau. Of course. Her passport would inform her, with complete authority, how old she was. Her passport, poor thing, had a function after all.

But her thoughts didn't stop there. Her thoughts pressed round her with sudden insistence.

She had got out of bed. 'Leapt' was a word she'd abandoned long ago. On the other hand, getting up wasn't a struggle. It was not quite six o'clock in the morning. But why waste the hours of a birthday? And she knew that her central heating—another faithful friend—would have clicked on at exactly 5.45.

All this displayed remarkable presence of mind. Yet there

was a general uncertainty that dogged her these days, of which not knowing her age was only an example. Was her mind going? That was the question. The answer might be: Of course not. Then it might be: Possibly. Or: Yes, and no. *She* wasn't going anywhere, but was her mind going? Increasingly, her answer to this question—and now, in the early hours of her birthday, she felt the heady whirl of it—was: She hoped so.

Her body, the thing that had now manoeuvred her quite nimbly out of bed, was still, at eighty-something, so remarkably intact and reliable, though at the same time remarkably withered and ugly, that she'd begun to think that it *must* be her mind that would go first. Loss of mind was, also, a much recognised symptom of age. Some feared it. She did not. She thought, in fact, that it might be a very convenient solution. The possibility that her mind might part company with her body and so not have to witness or suffer her body's eventual disintegration seemed a considerable mercy, and she waited, quite calmly, for the moment when her mind would say to her physical self, 'Goodbye, it's been nice knowing you, but you're on your own now.'

But then, if she could think such thoughts, how could her mind be going?

*

She opened the drawer of her bureau and felt inside. She hardly had to 'rummage'. She knew where it was. She held it, looked at it. Yes, it looked immaculate, as unblemished as on the day it was born. Its semi-stiff cover still had its original sheen and felt, beneath her fingers—unlike her own skin—uncreased and smooth. On the front was the gold coat of arms of the United Kingdom. It still shone. The cover seemed to want to open of itself onto pages that still emitted the odour of the freshly printed.

And there, on the all-important page, was the information she required. She was eighty-two, as she'd really suspected all along. Not eighty-one. She'd *been* eighty-one, she was now eighty-two. Next to the day and month of her date of her birth, was the startling number: 1937. Goodness me. With a little effort, she could still do her sums. It was 10th October 2019. She was pretty sure of that. And she was eighty-two.

Her mind was leaving her?

And her passport, she could work this out too, was a little over two years old. She was eighty years older than her passport. Goodness. And, incontestably, she must once have been two years old herself.

And, two years ago and more, she must have gone, determinedly, to a post office to collect a form, and then, possibly on the same conscientious trip, to the photo booth, just along from Sainsbury's in the shopping mall, where she must have sat, perfectly still, for all the world like some two-year-old child doing as she'd been told, waiting for the light to flash.

And here, before her now, was the result. Ugh! The face of a suspect, a convict. In any case, the face of a skull around which had been somehow moulded a coating of shrivelled flesh. And that had been two years ago.

What on earth had she thought of, sitting there in that booth? Why am I *doing* this? Do I *need* to do this? Or had she thought, dreamily, of all the places where she might go? Of all those immigration officers, in their own glassed-in booths, who would look at her passport, then at her, then, rather worryingly, back at the passport, but then, wearily, though perhaps with the flicker of a smile—for a harmless old lady—wave her through. You're free to go.

Free to go! To where she would reclaim her luggage and then be whisked away to some fabulous hotel.

All her life—most of her life—there had been a special journey that she'd wished and even vowed to make, but had never made. At some point it had dawned on her that there really was no way of travelling through time. Who was that little girl who'd just got out of bed?

But, yes, she must have gone into the booth, pulling the half-curtains quickly closed behind her, and read the instructions and inserted her coins. Anyone passing by must have seen her stick-like, eighty-year-old legs and her decidedly unfashionable shoes. They must have thought, if they were interested at all: There must be some old bat sitting in there.

Here was her passport. So might she still, at eighty-two, make the journey?

And there, next to the photo, was her name: 'Anna-Maria Alice Anderson'. She hadn't forgotten, at least, her own name. How could you forget such a parade of 'A's? And the hyphen, of course, the little, necessary hyphen. The passport authorities hadn't overlooked that. The print was small and, though it was new, quite hard to read. Her eyes were going, but only a bit. And there, properly placed, was the indelible fleck of the hyphen.

No, it's not Anna *and* Maria, or Anna *or* Maria. It's Anna-Maria. It's my name.

A hyphen. What would a hyphen be, if it were not a humble, barely visible punctuation mark? Some kind of mythical beast?

Once, long ago, she had been a schoolteacher. She might once even have said, 'schoolmistress', a word as antiquated as 'bureau'. Had she really been such a creature, standing before children—never having had any of her own—imparting to them her superior knowledge? Wisdom even.

Had she 'done' the hyphen with them, when they were doing punctuation, using, recklessly, herself as an example? Now they would all know that their teacher had this make-your-mind-up name. The hyphen was really very simple, it was just a link. It joined two items together, turning them into one. It was not half as complicated as the apostrophe. And what would the apostrophe be, if it were not an irritating punctuation mark? Some minor form of catastrophe?

Have I ever told you my story, children, the story of my life? There's the simple version and the complicated one. The simple one is very simple. I was orphaned. I am an orphan. For nearly eighty years now, I have been an orphan. I never knew my parents. I have no link with them. They died when I was very small.

But there's the complicated version.

I was born in October 1937, as my passport says. In London. My father's name was Michael Anderson, and he was from London, and my mother's name had been, till recently, Maria Ortega, and she was from Madrid. But in October 1937 they were both living in Walthamstow,

London. It might be simplest to say that I never knew either of them. But would it be true?

After I was orphaned, I was brought up by my father's older sister, my Auntie Joyce, and I certainly knew *her*—for fifteen years. She hated me. Or it might be fairer to say, I made her hate me, so I could hate *her* all the more. It was all about hating. From my Auntie Joyce I found out a little about my father and mother, but it was like getting blood from a stone, since I think my Aunt Joyce had come also to hate her brother and his Spanish wife—because a consequence of their cut-short lives was that I had been dumped on my aunt. But, in the circumstances—it was during a war and she lived in Hemel Hempstead, a safe but unexciting place—she could hardly refuse to take me in.

We hated each other, but this made it simple for me, when I reached my eighteenth birthday, to run away from my auntie. I ran away with a man called George—George Grayson—and never saw Aunt Joyce again. To make sure of my new life with George, I soon married him. To have made it doubly sure, I might have got pregnant first—a common ploy. But George married me anyway, and it was only later that we found out that I *couldn't* get pregnant, that we couldn't have children. But George had married me anyway.

None of this sounds very romantic—though 'running away' sounds romantic. None of it sounds much like love. But I think George and I loved each other, in our way. We were married for twenty-five years, and it can't be easy to be married to an orphan who can't, herself, have children. Nor, perhaps, is it easy to be an orphaned daughter who can't be a mother, and who has spent all her girlhood years with her Auntie Joyce.

But then George ran away, himself. He ran away from me. Was this because he was, by then, forty-something and wanted the children I couldn't give him, or because he wanted the younger woman who was then, apparently, on offer? Both things, perhaps. I found out that her name was April. April! I'll never know how it worked out with George and April. He went out of my life, and I don't know, now, if he's even in the land of the living. He ran away at least twice in his life, once with me and once with April.

I think it's something that quite a few people do at least once in their lives. You may do it yourselves, children, one day, though it's not for me to recommend it. There comes a point when people run away. They want to put the life that they have behind them and find another one. They want, even, to become another person. Little boys, in old stories, used to run away to sea. And I think it's what my father,

Michael Anderson, did. He ran away to Spain, and then my mother ran away—back again—with him.

But I don't blame George for running away from me, though it's easy to say that now. I don't blame him. He was not a bad man, and we had all those years together. During those years I became a teacher, and when I became a teacher George gave me the biggest, most generous and most memorable birthday present I've ever had. Though 'memorable' is hardly the right word, since, unlike so many things, it's not a thing of memory. I'm sitting at it right now. A bureau.

But it makes me remember George.

He must have got it from some second-hand furniture place. Even so, it must have cost him. It's walnut, with brass handles to the drawers, and at the back, above the desk, are lots of little niches and shelves. It was not a present George was able to keep as a surprise, but it's the best and most useful present I've ever had. And it's still here, unlike George. He said that if I was going to be a teacher, then I should have a desk of my own at home, for my own homework.

I cried, children. Your teacher cried. Imagine that. And I hugged him.

But it didn't stop him walking out on me many years

277

later. I was left alone, when I was forty-something myself, and, despite some fumbling and wasted efforts over the years to find some other 'companion in life'—I won't go into that poorly punctuated story—it's how it's been ever since. Alone, but with a bureau for companion.

And if I'm sitting here alone at my bureau, even if it's my 'teacher's' bureau, then I don't know how I can be talking to you, children. I haven't been in a classroom for over twenty years. I wouldn't know what a school's like these days. So I'm talking to you as if you're the kids I taught all those years ago and you're now just somewhere in the air. It's a bit like talking to my parents.

She sat, holding her passport, like some newly opened birthday present. In her hand it seemed to tingle at the oddity of being touched. She would get no other birthday present today, she was pretty sure of that. No cards had, so far, come through the letter box. Would there be a deluge this morning? She ran her fingers over the passport's smooth surface, thumbed the still pristine pages. A birthday present to herself.

'Anna-Maria Alice Anderson.'

Yes, her parents were somewhere in the air. That's how she thought of them. How else could she think of them?

They were ghosts fluttering somewhere in the air. And so they might flutter over her and even *see* her, though she couldn't see them. Perhaps they were doing so right now.

My God, can that be our little Anna-Maria? She looks ancient. And she's holding what looks like a passport.

And *they* must still be the age that they were when they died. So when she 'saw' them, or thought she saw them, in her mind, it was like seeing *her* children. Or grandchildren. Or great-grandchildren . . .

Was her mind going? She hoped so. She hoped it would hurry up and just go.

Outside, it was still dark. It was October. And quiet. She supposed that, though dark, the sky was clear. The makings, perhaps, of some brilliant crisp autumn day, specially for her.

But not quiet, not quiet at all. She could hear, up above, the steady decelerating whine of planes, in procession, one becoming audible as the other faded, making their descents into Heathrow. It would start at about 5 a.m. It was so familiar that, usually, she didn't notice it. She noticed it now. If she were to go to the window, pull back the curtains and crane her neck, she might see the blinking lights. In each of those planes there were passengers, and each one of those passengers must have a passport with them. Otherwise, they couldn't be there.

But she stayed at her bureau, in a pool of light from a lamp, bent studiously over the rare object she'd taken from the drawer. Once, she recalled, passports had declared not only who you were, but what you were, what you did. Her previous passports would never have said 'Orphan', though it was a kind of life's occupation, but they must have said 'Teacher'. As a primary-school teacher, she must have taught some rudimentary history, but, now she was so much older, she wondered if she might have become a historian. And her passport might then have said—quite impressively—'Historian'.

But how absurd. What an absurd word even: 'historian'. Was it a job? A profession? An attitude? Yet the thing about being a historian, so she imagined, was that you could 'rise above'. You might see things, looking down, as from some special aeroplane, as her parents might be looking down on her now.

If she were a historian, she might, for example, say of her father, Michael Anderson, not that he'd met her mother, Maria Ortega, in Madrid, but that 'he was present at the siege of Madrid'. Or that 'he took part in the battle for Madrid'. As if he might not have been her father at all.

But she was not a historian. How ridiculous. She sometimes wasn't sure if she'd ever been a schoolteacher. Was that really *her*? She'd begun, in recent years, to catch herself using in her head an expression that, generally, she despised: 'in another life'. How ridiculous. 'In another life' she was a schoolteacher. 'In another life' she might have been a historian.

What nonsense. In another life she might have been a film star. There was only one life, the one you had.

She was Anna-Maria Alice Anderson. She had, at least, that drumroll of a name. After George skedaddled, she had reinstated the surname of her father. She had a name and a bureau and central heating and a passport. She was not doing badly.

In 1936, children, my father ran away to Spain. That's one way of putting it, but another, more historical way might be to say that, as a young man, still not much more than a boy, he'd felt urged to go to Spain, to pick up a rifle and fight the fascists. To fight General Franco. Why should a boy from Walthamstow have wanted to go and fight in Spain? I don't know. But, no doubt, his parents and his big sister Joyce disapproved, and might even have washed their hands of him. Was his mother called Alice?

But things turned out better than he'd hoped—whatever he'd hoped—since he'd met his future wife, Maria Ortega, and brought her back, after only a few months, to Walthamstow. And she must have been ready to be brought back by him, to do some running away herself. And this was because—never mind General Franco and the Spanish Civil War—they were madly in love.

Or that's what I believe. That's what I've believed all my life.

And they also brought back me. Some homework—a little history, arithmetic and biology—have taught me that I must have been conceived, perhaps even amid the sound of explosions, in Spain. I, too, must have been present, in an invisible way, at the siege of Madrid. Imagine that.

But I was born in October 1937 in Walthamstow. And I must have got my double-barrelled first name, not a common English custom, from my mother, because, perhaps, *her* mother's name was Anna, and her own name was Maria. My parents were going to live in England, but their child was to have a Spanish name and a double one. A fair deal. And the 'Alice' must have been my father's choice.

But one night in December 1940, not long after my third birthday, in what was known as the Blitz, a bomb fell on the house in Walthamstow where I was with my mother, though we should have been in some shelter, and my mother was killed, though I, by some combination of miracle and disaster of which I have no memory, survived, unharmed.

My father was not there, because he was, once again, fighting the fascists. This time, it was Mussolini, in Africa. But what neither I nor my mother knew on that December night (though my Aunt Joyce would later tell me) was that he'd already been killed, in Egypt.

In a history book it might say, 'He lost his life in the defence of Egypt against the Italian army.' And of my mother, 'She lost her life during the London Blitz.' As if they'd never met each other and fallen madly in love.

But I would have known nothing, in any case, of any of this. I was barely three. It was before I had a memory. I have no memory of a bomb whistling down on a house in Walthamstow and killing my mother but not me, and perhaps that's just as well. And I've sometimes thought that if I'd died with my mother, then I would have had no memory of ever being alive, it would have been as though I'd never existed.

But here I am, aged eighty-two.

I've sometimes thought, too, that, since my mother died without ever knowing that my father, her husband, had been killed—something she must have feared from the moment he went off to fight (a second time)—and since my father would never have known of my mother's death, then, in that sense, they were both spared. It was as though they'd died together.

And I was spared, but not spared. Since at the age of three, without knowing anything, I became an orphan.

I've sometimes also wondered if it might not have been best if all three of us had died together. And I've sometimes had the further thought that none of us is supposed to have—and what a thought to be putting before you: Suppose I had never been born.

But life is cruel, children, you will find this. I am your teacher, and let me not hide it from you. If life turns out to be short, well then that's cruel. But when life is long, that can be cruel too. When people say: oh, she or he had a good life, a good long life; when people talk about how we're all living longer these days, how longevity's a fine thing in itself, a gift of our modern times—don't be fooled. Should you ever get to eighty or eighty-one, let alone eighty-two, and people should say to you—if they talk to you or notice you at all—if they should say, cheerily and well-meaningly, 'But you're *only* eighty . . .' then you'll understand what I mean.

My parents died young, and good for them. Do I shock you? They will always be in their youth. They will always have the glow of their brevity, and their bravery. They met and they lived under conditions of brevity and bravery. Is it brave just to count the endless years?

I was orphaned at the age of three. I was ditched by George when I was forty-something. I should know about counting the years, and I should know about being alone. But the trouble with counting the years is that sooner or later—you lose count. And the trouble with living to a ripe old age and being still, amazingly, though you're a bag of bones, quite good on your pins and able to go to Sainsbury's and carry back something to eat so you can keep on clocking up the years, is that it all gets very repetitive and tedious—and you get more and more *alone*.

How do I know that my parents had their glow and their bravery, if they died when I was three, before I had a memory? Well, you tell me, children. You're much nearer to three than I am. But here's a question for you from your ancient teacher, a rather tricky question, though it's not a trick question: How can we remember that we *didn't* have a memory? And is it true that the memories that I sometimes *think* I have—now that I'm old and my mind's going—are only imaginary, only my old mind playing tricks?

They say that we remember everything. *Everything.* It's all still there. It's just that we don't have the key, the passport. Who was that little girl who got out of bed?

She moved from the chair at the bureau to her nearby armchair, her passport still firmly grasped in her hand. She settled where she'd settled so often before. Her bureau, her armchair—two companions for life. But, this time, she settled with a certain facing-forward, braced expectancy, as people do on an aeroplane when it's about to take off.

And now she remembered again the little round metal seat in the photo booth that you were instructed to adjust to the right height. She remembered making sure that her head and shoulders were correctly positioned, that she was staying still and not blinking or—God forbid—smiling.

Outside, there was still the sound of the planes. They were landing, not taking off. Once, in London, long ago, everyone would have heard the sound of bombers.

And now she remembered when she was only two, *exactly* two. She could remember nothing? She could remember it all. She was getting out of bed again. She was very small and light. She barely knew how to walk. It was dark. But, if she didn't know yet what a 'birthday' was, she'd been told the day before that this would be a very special day for her. So she'd woken early, excited, wanting to get up and meet this special day.

It was dark, but across the landing was a beckoning light. She tottered towards her parents' bedroom. She'd swayed on tiny, soft legs, so unlike the brittle things beneath her in the photo booth.

The door was ajar, a light was on inside. She'd heard them talking in low voices. She didn't know this, but it must have been before, though not so long before, her father had gone off to fight again. It was October 1939.

And there he was, inside the bedroom, his back to her, standing before a dressing-table mirror. He'd just put on a shirt. He might have glimpsed her—in the mirror—standing in the gap of the just-opened door, but he'd moved forward, stooping to see better what he was doing and so had blocked out her reflection. And she had stayed in the doorway.

He was struggling with a collar and a collar stud—she understood this now. It was his daughter's birthday, but he still had some kind of work to go to. He didn't have to pick up another rifle, not quite yet.

She stood, watching him, and all at once her mother, in a white nightdress, her back also turned, had moved up behind him and quickly helped him with the collar. They were busy with each other, unaware of her. They'd never know she was there, looking. It might have been some room in Madrid.

Her mother lingered close behind her father, pressing against him, and, with one hand on his shoulder, she ran a finger slowly along the gap of flesh between the collar and his hair. Then she kissed the same narrow band of skin. She ran her lips, even more slowly, along it, like someone licking the envelope of a precious letter. She kissed the nape of his neck. She seemed to want to eat it. And she whispered something.

In the doorway, she could hear it. She couldn't have understood it. It was in a foreign language. But *all* language, then, for her, was a kind of foreign language. And it was also in a kind of child's language.

She couldn't remember it? She hadn't been there? She was anyway just an unseen reflection, a little ghost, in a mirror.

It was whispered, but she heard it. She heard it now, as then. She'd had eighty years to understand it and to recognise, again and again, her mother's under-her-breath voice.

'*Miguelito . . .*'

*

Oh, they'd been madly in love. She knew it. So did she really need to go on this impossible journey, to rediscover what she already knew?

But she sat, facing forward, gripping her passport. Her bureau was all on its own now.

What they don't tell you, children, is that you get to a point when another year, another birthday means nothing, it adds nothing, you've had enough. And yet you're still here, less and less of you, but still here, and apparently immortal. It just won't do.

It was October 2019. Was her mind going? Well, let it go. Wave me through, please. Not another year, please. She'd lasted for so many of them, and the world, it seemed, had nothing specially lined up for her, either to whisk her away or to detain her.

So she'd just have to go.

It was 6.30 a.m. Still dark. She sat, looking forward, braced and prepared, clutching the proof of her identity, but she was really somewhere else already and she knew, as well as she ever would, who she was.

She sat and she waited. She waited. She waited for the light to flash.

ACKNOWLEDGEMENTS

Grateful acknowledgements are made to the publications in which the following stories, reprinted here with some revisions, first appeared:

'The Next Best Thing': *The Telegraph* and, in German translation, *Süddeutsche Zeitung*

'Blushes', 'Fireworks', 'Hinges', 'Bruises': *The New Yorker*

'Beauty': *The Atlantic*